AUTOENDOBIOGRAPHICAL:
THE BOOK THAT
NEVER ENDS

Autoendobiographical: The Book That Never Ends

iUniverse books may be ordered through booksellers or by contacting:

iUniverse
1663 Liberty Drive
Bloomington, IN 47403
www.iuniverse.com
1-800-Authors (1-800-288-4677)

ISBN: 978-1-4759-2271-4 (sc)
ISBN: 978-1-4759-2272-1 (ebk)

Printed in the United States of America

iUniverse rev. date: 05/17/2012

AUTOENDOBIOGRAPHICAL:
THE BOOK THAT
NEVER ENDS

BRENTON PLOURDE

iUniverse, Inc.
Bloomington

WORKS CITED

Perincic, Natalija. *Older Sister is a Friend*. Edmonton: Croatian Press, 2012.

Guthrie, Anna. *Stick With Me Baby*. Detroit: Guthrie Publishing, 2008.

Hiebert, Crystal. *Paid in Full*. Calgary: Mennonite Publishing 2012.

Plourde, Cindy, and Brian Plourde. *Parental Control*. Orillia: Plourde Publishing, 1976.

This is the book that never ends. It's not that I am not a good writer; it's just that this book will never end.

I also have decided not to indent. Why indent? You know that previous sentence is the beginning of a new paragraph.

So the idea of a never ending book came to me the other day while I was reading a book that did end. I sometimes feel when reading a book and it ends that I would not have ended the book that way at all? I mean who cares if he lives and his family is all around him as he is the hospital, broken arms and broken legs and broken dreams but the love and the warmth of his family will bring him through?

There are books that do allow you to end them the way you would. They are called "Choose Your Own Adventure" but again you are asked to turn to page 72 if you feel Sally should follow the strange sound she hears as she investigates the death of Mrs. Johnston's cat or turn to page 165 if you think that Sally should call the police. The cat died and I am sure Mrs. Johnston is upset but at 86, she should get over it and well is close to death herself, so think of it as a pre-requisite to where she is going.

The World Association of Girl Guides and Girl Scouts (WAGGGS) motto is always "Be Prepared."

So even if you choose not to make a choice and do nothing, you have still made a choice. Go ahead, stop reading this never ending book now, put it down, shelve it or even take it to your local used bookstore and trade it in for Stephen King—I personally don't care, this book never ends anyways.

I plan on making literary history with this book. This is the Bible for the "new generation". Forget Coupland and his "Gen X" bullshit of the early 1990s—this is the 2000s and we are "Gen Why?" I have to go to work—why? I have to pay my cell phone bill—why? I have to listen to what my parents say and be home by 11:30 p.m.—why?

So following that formula and hard core logo above, why does this book have to end? Us "Gen Why-ers?" are just going to shrug our shoulders when asked by "the man" to do something that we do not want to do and then go play XBOX or Nintendo Wii or go skateboarding at the local Gulp and Slurp on a Saturday night.

Even though the next page in common sense thinking would be page two, in fact it is whatever page number you want it to be. Make it page 17, make it page 142. I have no idea how many pages or made up fictional pages this never ending book will have.

Speaking of fiction - You know when people say a joke is 50% a joke and 50% the truth, isn't fiction like that as well? Jack Kerouac hung out with Neal Cassady for a year or so and wrote his book—yet it is titled as fiction—made up, a story, not real but it was real. Sure the names where changed and maybe some of the backgrounds but 50% of that book (actually probably like 90%) is real but yet they classify it as "fiction". Why not just call it "realitiction".

I have always wanted to be an actor. I have watched a lot of movies and have my favorite actors. Everyday I act. That's right, everyday I act like I care or am amused or am loving. I think I would take the direct opposite approach or "Bassackwards" to acting and to life. You always hear how the actor would wonder how his or her character would do a scene or how they would feel in a certain scene. To me, I would incorporate this into my everyday life but do it backwards. How would my character play me in real life? How would Sam Winston (the character in the movie) play Brenton J. Plourde in real life? Would Sam Winston not cry when his dog had to be put asleep? Would Brenton J. Plourde do that in real life? Let Sam Winston—the character—worry about how he would deal with death, love and life in the real life of Brenton J. Plourde.

I find nothing entertaining in the Entertainment section of my local newspaper.

Devised plan. On Saturday afternoons I hangout in the local Walk—In Clinic in my town. I sit and flip through the magazines from last year, reading about who won the Super Bowl last year and how great I can look if I lose that extra 15 lbs if I really applied myself at that time last year and be slimmer and more desirable at this time, one year from then. So I go there every Saturday afternoon and watch (secret agent man like) as the girls my age come in and take those pamphlets on certain diseases and how and what you can do to prevent it then I make mental notes to stay away from those ones when I see them at the club later on that night.

The bus always smells. We need bus fresheners. I also like reading yesterday's newspaper on the bus or subway. I wonder who brought this newspaper on here? Were they shocked when they found out the mother murdered that little girl in the East End? Did they snicker to themselves when they found a certain celebrity got into trouble again? The abandoned Sudoku or Crossword is always good—17 down—three letters—Baseball player Mel ___.

I reached into my pocket, pulled out my pen, filled in "Ott" and put the paper down on the seat beside me and pulled the string. The bell rang and I got off. Good bye newspaper, my three letters "Ott" was my contribution to your life.

I have always wanted to write a short story based on the 1942 Edward Hopper painting *Nighthawks*. So I took seven minutes and wrote this:

3

I did not have the heart to tell Lisa I was not a detective. I sit in this café with my detective hat on and my detective jacket on and back towards the window—my back towards the world.

The couple at the bar does not look like a couple at all. The man, who dresses like me, seems to be off in the distance. I wonder if he is a fake detective like me. The red dress the woman is wearing is nice but it does not flatter her one bit. It is just past 2 A.M. and it feels late.

From what I cannot hear, there is no one on the street. The streets are always quiet at this time. People do not seem to go out anymore. They are all nestled in, listening to the radio or watching television.

The man in the white seems to be enthralled with their conversation. He looks twice as old as me and appears to have been working here three times as long. I bet that man has heard it all from fights with wives and girlfriends to how the Brooklyn Dodgers are going to win the World Series. The day the coffee gets any better in this place, the Dodgers will win the World Series.

I did not have the heart to tell Lisa I was not a detective. I am merely an out of work actor playing a detective in my mind. From one audition to another, I try and "detect" if I have even the slightest chance passing the audition to play a detective on those new detective

4

shows on television. For reasons I do not know, I still have no "clue."

I will admit it could be better but then again, so could I and well so could you. Where people gain their inspirations to write things is purely based on how they feel or what triggers then at the time. I personally have one trigger and that trigger will remain my secret as if I told you then you will trigger yourself then write your own book and no one will buy this one.

Over the last however long it has been, I have been writing other stuff aside from this. So I decided to include the other stuff here purely for filler. These are all organized by day that I wrote them. There are spaces between each piece so you will know where the end and the beginning begin.

Sunday November Thirteenth Two Thousand Eight

According to Microsoft Word, this is Document 6. Now normally I would not think too much of this announcement by Microsoft Word but it struck a cord with me. How many times has Microsoft Word made this announcement to me? Why was I not notified during Document 5 that Document 6 is just around the corner?

To Microsoft and the Microsoft Word Company, I suggest you get that little "Paperclip Guy" to start announcing Document 6—it would save me a lot of stress.

You know what George Michael said to me? He said "I Want Your Sex." I am not sure if I am ready to give it to him yet.

I did not want to give you a clue. I wanted you to sit and wonder why I was so discouraged. Today was a special day. Not another Sunday—not even any given Sunday. It has some significance. God, who generally takes Sunday off, made a point of leaving me a "Happy Birthday Buddy!" on my Facebook page.

Made a fire and watching it burn. The fire I am watching burn exists in no fireplace and no campfire but many of these fires have started there.

The burning fire is for you. I hoped to kindle my heart with "IHopeSheWould" logs and the special "IKnowIWould" logs, which according to the package burns longer and brighter than the previously mentioned logs, in order to rekindle some night time fire side romance with you.

This fire has now died down.

There are no more logs.

Toasted marshmallow emotions.

My hands are sticky.

I rub them on my pants.

I rub my eyes.

My tears seem to have put out what was left of the embers.

Extinguish.

I called the operator and she told me the time was now.

The trees dance dark shadows. I can barely see them but I know they are there. One minute they are calm and the next they are not. It is as if they are either trying to get my attention and warn me about the storm that is coming or distract me from my writing with their interpretation of "Walk Like an Egyptian".

We all learn. We all learn from our mistakes and other people's short comings. One could write a book on how we learn from mistakes—Mistakes for Dummies.

That last little line there was obvious, no? Mistakes for Dummies. Kinda was self obvious on that one, again another mistake—Mistake for Dummy.

I fail to see any mistakes in my life so far. I do not think of them as mistakes but as "Eventual Non Do-Overs" in my mind. I have my own YouTube page in my head and everyday I post all my "Eventual Non Do-Overs" on it, generally they only run close to a minute.

There is only one subscriber to my YouTube page and that is me. Sometimes I lie in my bed at night and play all the videos and laugh and leave comments in the comment areas, things like "LOL" or "Great! Did you see the way the milk came out my nose! Classic!"

> Someone once told me it was easy to fall in love. Someone once told me it was easy to fall out of love. Someone once told me not to listen to those two someone's as they had no idea what they were talking about.
> I chose a different route. I followed my heart. I did not care what road it took and how many stop lights it took, I wanted the journey and that journey wanted me—I could feel it. My left signal may have been on the whole time, but I did not care.

The very thought of her. The very thought of her. The very thought of her. The very thought. The very of her. Her.

Some people say you reach a crossroads in the journey to find love. I did not. My journey was already mapped out before hand: I Google Love Mapped It and printed it out before I left. It said that if I followed this red line and went 789 miles, I would reach my destination by five years. My printer seems to be running out of ink. I seem to be running out of time.

Yes, there were some roadside attractions. I stopped to taste the pie and to pick the berries but my basket was full already. My inner basket was full of fruitful thoughts of her. She was like the pie that was just taken out of the oven and put on the window sill, you can just see it—the curtains gently fan the 'hotness' as the wind pushes them back and forth.

Roadside attractions. Roadside attractions. Roadside Attracts.

Storm coming in. Sometimes I see people on television, on those shows that have couples who are not getting along and they are like the weather on the your local news. You can see how just twenty-four hours ago there was sunshine, clear skies, no need to wear long pants—shorts weather I would say. Then in a second, you can see the relationship storms moving in—cold front by her, thunder by him. You know that there will always be sunshine again but given the fact the weatherman is never right - your Las Vegas odds are slim to none.

Two hundred miles left. Two years left. Two fries left. Two times I looked at her picture within the last minute.

The roadway drives me to silence, reflection and tunnel vision ponder. Would she be the same as I imagined her 5 years ago? Would she still say "de-ton-inating" instead of "detonating"? I have a feeling this may blow up in my face. It is 6:08 P.M. and judging my watch, she is just 2 minutes away from not home.

Thursday December Fourth Two Thousand Eight

I believe. I believe in you. In you I believe. You believe in I. In I you believe. Believe I.

In the evening. A quiet hysteria. With my windows closed, I can still hear the trees, with help from the wind, whispering about me. What right do they have? They do not know me? Who are they to judge?

I have high endurance, you know. I would run the "Jillian Marathon of Hope". I would pass all the runners, boyfriend #6 and lover #23 and come in first at the Finish Line only to discover that I had been disqualified for loving someone else.

Prelude. It has been awhile since we spoke last. I wanted to tell you how I felt and I wanted to do it fast.

Emotion. Like a sugar rush from eating too many sugar filled candies or nine packets of sugar in my coffee. I wanted to tell you how I felt and I wanted to do it fast.

Discouragement. You looked at me with wonderment. You scrunched your eyes until that little line was on your forehead. I wanted you and I wanted to do it.

Horizon. Like John Wayne in every cowboy movie, when his job was done and the town was saved. You were gone. How I felt wanted fast.

The Red Light District was full of red lights but I did not stop. Girls danced in the windows and men stopped to watch, rooting through their pockets for that last twenty dollars for a quick delight. I did not watch the girls, I watched men's eyes, how they watched the girls and how they glanced side to side, to see who was coming—wives or girlfriends or Mothers, looking for their sons who were not old enough to be there. I must admit I did look at one of the girls, but all I could think of was you—Her name is Jillian and I wanted to hook[h]er.

This is the part when the instrumental comes in.

We lead a renaissance. We do what we want and when we want. We scream when there is silence and we sleep when it is daytime. People look at us funny but we do not care. They will teach about us from their History textbooks. They will write about us, a classroom full of students will have write two thousand words on us, MLA Format.

Don't write what you know—know what you write. They should teach that in school. It would make life so much easier for Journalists all around the world. Right what you know—know what you right.

Sunday December Seventh Thousand Eight

Another
Nights
Dream

Reassures
Exact
Attraction

I hear them arguing on the front lawns in the summer evenings. Every night it's always the same things. Fights of trust and confrontations with claws out and "backs up." Those damn cats, get off my lawn you pussies, I am trying to sleep.

I saw you crying yesterday. I did not know what to say. I wanted to tell you it would be okay. I wanted to tell you that I understood. I wanted to give you a hug and gently position you to look me in the eyes and wipe away your tears with my thumb. I let the Kleenex do my talking.

I spread my arms as wide as they can. This is how much I love you. You look at me in amazement. You, for the first time in your life, feel wanted. I try and stretch my fingers out a bit more. You run to me and gently wrap your arms around me, your head on my breast. I stand with my arms still wide open—you close your eyes. Your arms still wrapped around me—hug me tight. This is how much you love me.

My band was formed in 1976. I write all the songs and play all the instruments—live in concert and on the records. I tour for 12 months a year. Not every show is sold out but it is a living. I just wish people would light their BIC Lighters when my "teen anthem" is played live. I extend the guitar solo. My life is a concert and it is controlled improvisation.

People say I have a keen sense of visuals. I do not see that. I do not think in 3-D nor do I see things in different lights. I just simply understand stuff differently than the next person. I can not tell you the future nor can I tell you the past but I do know one thing: You will have a headache within the next two years.

These are my eyes. I close my eyes and think of eternal sunshine. I open them and darkness falls upon me. These are my eyes. They are blue and they see right through me.

Mold me. Make me who you want me to be. Change me, bend me, offend me but do it gently. I am your Stretch Armstrong. Dress me, obsesses me, suppress me but do it comfortably. I am your Ken Doll. Use your illusion one and two. Dust N' Bones. Civil War.

Your silence does not speak louder than words. It is quiet in here. The quiet is too loud for me. I turn up the stereo. This song makes me happy. It reminds me of the times we spent quiet evenings together.

Monday December Eighth Two Thousand Eight

David Gray is hoping this years love better last—me too my friend, sounds like you need this right now. Do not worry Dave, John Mayer and I are still waiting on the world to change.

I was Ethan Hawke before Ethan Hawke was Ethan Hawke. Sorry Mr. Hawke, this is true and well I know this Reality Bites.

Just her
Innocent
Little
Love
I
Absolutely
Need

The garbage man told me you cannot throw away a broken heart—you have to recycle it.

The snow falls straightly vertical. Every flake travels in slow motion. No wind, no essence of time what so ever. A red car passes.

Footprints of a travel to somewhere by someone two hours ago are on the sidewalk. I am looking out my window. I want to grab hold of each side of the window frame and shake the outside world—like a snow globe.

You are one throw rug in the den away from being perfect.

Tuesday December Tenth Two Thousand Eight

My humble pie does not taste as good as your humble pie. Mine needs I scream.

Subconsciously I try not to let you get to me.
Subconsciously I try not to let you get to me.

The ironic thing about Alanis Morissette is that she probably would go down on you in the theatre.

This is another one of those deep and meaningless epics. The ones that are always filled with clichés like you sit in your oriel and look out at the stars and the moon and wonder what I am doing and if I am thinking of you and I lay upon my bed with my hands behind me bed wondering the same.

This is filled with me hanging up right before you pick up the phone and you thinking you see me across the street, going to into a café and when you get there, even though it was not me, "I" am gone.

This is me with a picture of you as my wallpaper on my phone and you like to think that even though I am across town, across Canada or across the world, that you are what I want and what I need. You know exactly what you would wear and say and how you would end our "day together" if we met.

We have our own song. It is Peter Gabriel's "In Your Eyes". You picked it out because you like the lyrics. I stand with my ghetto blaster over my head outside your window. For almost 5 minutes I am Lloyd Dobler and you are Diane Court.

This is another one of those deep and meaningless epics. With the pen you gave me, I wrote this.

Wednesday December Tenth Two Thousand Eight

Just past one and the clock moves at a slow pace, slower than usual. Afternoon self selected jazz on the turntable does not move me the way it was first intended. The coffee machine percolates distant thunder and offers a sweet smell of success. Phone set to "Andrea" but it does not make a sound.

I ask myself, "Why am I not sweeping you up off your feet at the Emerald Ball"? Instead I am sweeping up around everyone's feet the Emerald Bar, just down on Main St. Just past one and the clock moves at a slower pace, slower than usual. Early morning broom time, it's late and all I can think of is you.

I turn my bracelet round and round and I recall my mind Polaroid. Phone set to "Andrea" but it does not make a sound. No planes are flying out of Pearson and the Niagara Falls is silent tonight.

Bus stop romance
Coffee shop side glance
Hallway crossroads
Walk you to your class—Your books I do carry.

Phone font conversation
Written, verbal demonstration
Friday night congregation
Your stomach flutters—butterfly sanctuary.

The very thought of you
Makes me happy as the day is long.

I do not want to say the snow covered the yard like a giant white
blanket
No one would care if I opened the window and cried wolf
People will tell you that life is what you make it
I look at my made bed and wonder when the next time
Someone will share it with me
My hands have lost their tan
My heart has lost that loving feeling
A little boy is delivering the newspaper
It is close to 8 p.m.
I go downstairs to look at the Personals.
I know that I cannot reply. You ask me to exemplify, justify and
realize. I sit and stare at out window. My hand wants to touch yours.
I want turn to you and tell you how I feel. I want to. Emotional
Ocean. Currents are current. I died in the water.
My internal calendar says three weeks
My external calendar says the same
I circled the date
When I get to use your name
To your face, when I tell you how much I missed you.
I want to store all these great feelings and times
Relationship memorabilia
In your Love Hall of Fame.

Single lamp assures a shadowed night
8:34 P.M., head phoned slow ballad
On the radio
Verticals on the window pulled to reveal
Horizontal trees
Wearing white after Labor Day
And like his big brother sunshine
The moon pays no attention
The stars, they constellation your face
This bed is too big without you.

The turned on desk lamp sheds no light into what is bothering me
My heart, like a woman in chains, shifts not so violently
Like a woman on her last few breaths before she is about to give up
The shadow people sit still in the shadows
Waiting for the clock to strike midnight
For when they will run silently
The moon peaks in on me from time to time
To make sure I am okay
A car in the distance
Passes by my curtain opened window
The quickness makes me believe it has somewhere important to be
Like the messenger on the horse who has just learned of war
His hair flows in the wind, the horse gallops like there is no
tomorrow
For the messenger, there might not be
Bill Evans modally plays "Waltz for Debby" on the turntable
My heart gallops like there is no tomorrow
For me, there might not be.

With help from the wind, the trees throw winter confetti upon us
It is as if the whole world was celebrating our love
We kiss and you run across the street to catch your 52 seat chariot
I turn
To see your back
But your scarf wind waves "bye" to me
9:12 pm and the bus is right on time
Right on time for once, all I ask tonight is for one minute lateness.

Okay so I mentioned a few pages ago that I would not mention
what triggers me to write but well I guess I am going to go against
that statement and tell you: music.

I just flip on some music and the trigger fires. These next things
(for pure filler purposes as well this is the book that never ends so I
need to stretch this out for as long as I can) are based on jazz albums
by the Dave Brubeck Quartet (Ed. Note—the "classic quartet" is

where it is at. Dave Brubeck, Paul Desmond, Eugene Wright and Joe Morello from 1959 to 1967 is where you want to be).

Jazz Impressions of New York 1965.

Tracks:
01 - Theme From 'Mr. Broadway' [02:31]
02 - Broadway Bossa Nova [03:17]
03 - Autumn in Washington Square [05:31]
04 - Something to Sing About [03:57]
05 - Sixth Sense [06:58]
06 - Spring In Central Park [02:30]
07 - Lonely Mr. Broadway [04:21]
08 - Summer On The Sound [02:43]
09 - Winter Ballad [02:45]
10 - Broadway Romance [05:52]
11 - Upstage Rumba [04:20]

These are all order the same as they are order as the track listing. Also you will notice that there are words that are in bold though out each one. When read or put together from top to bottom they make a sentence that has something to do with the piece as a whole

This is the working hour. I cannot fathom any other way to tell you this. Put down your New Yorkers you New Yorkers—this is **the working hour**.

Find out what it is all about. It is all about location, location, location and your location to find out **is not here**. I say this is the working hour and you need to find out what it is all about and you only have one working hour.

Paperclip it to you heart, staple it to your mind. Verbal slideshow for others, make verbal copies in the verbal copier room **on the third floor**.

You will be strong. It is a daily planet and you are on it. This is the working hour and you will find out what it is all about—**you will be strong**.

Henri Salvador used to sing to me. I was young, when I **wanted to drown** my sorrow and there was **no tomorrow**, he was there—he was Mon voyage dans le Bonheur.

Fall. Fall to. Fall **to** the. Fall to the ground. Fall to the ground I. Fall to the ground I say. Tell me how it feels. Feel how it tells **me**.

The bench was cold. I sit in isolation right beside an old man with bread in hands; all torn up like **his** heart—the world's smallest sandwiches for the birds.

Pharaohs. They speak to me—no wait, those voices are the life people passing me by. It's not the art of **noise** it's the noise of art the old man tells me. He has painted me a picture of what I will be—its not still life as his hands move, it's life still—no movement for me when I reach his number of years **achieved** in this daily planet.

In his eyes I see **resolution**. My eyes camera **slowly** ascends towards the sky. Fin(e).

She is **gone**.

I believe in what is written in history books. **I do not believe** in black and white photographs—staged **in 1959** for our benefit.

Everyone looks off to the side—they do not look at me. I do not feel safe as I do when I look into someone's eyes—they give me pale shelter.

They don't give me love.

Listen. **I hear** all the concerts that were ever played here—sit. They all go in my ear as **one sound** but come out individually. Up and down, I catalogue them in my b-pod. One folder is labeled music and another is labeled music and another is labeled music.

I hear the crowds. **I hear** the lighters being flicked open and see the Flames of Albion burning brightly. The drummer plays the drums and the guitarist guitars and the singer sings. If these trees could **talk**, they would make me write down all the lyrics, correctly.

Checklist:
One towel
One toilet
One bathtub
One mirror
One toothbrush
One bed
One dresser
One desk
One chair
One window
One **New** York
One blinking red porno sign
One **man**
One vision.

The sun always shines on TV. The sun always shines in my window. I pull the curtains across the window and wait three minutes and open them again—it's like I changed the channel, the curtain is my remote—I go from the news of the world to an infomercial in a three minute curtain call—the sound is always fading in and out—Turn it up please! Turn it down please!

At night, my shows are in black and white. My window TV always has happy endings as the heroes all ride off into the sunset—horizon hold.

The sun always shines on TV. When the winter comes and the snow begins to fall, it's like how it snows on TV when the cable is out. **I try** my curtain remote but **it's all the same**, on every channel. I cannot wait for summer—**I** may move away, a **different** town—more channels, pay per view.

The snowball sailed **through** the air. The sound of calming violins. Danger! Danger! My eyes watch in **anticipation**. Like one does when watching Beckett's Act Without Words. Boom! Crash! Boom! The intending was **intended**. Like distant drums drumming in the distant. I waited for Godot—and it **came**.

I would buy her flowers but I decided to trace my hand on a piece of white paper from the copier room on the third floor. On each finger I drew four bubble petals around them and colored in the fingernails—sunflower on Carnation Street.

She sits silently, waiting for someone to message her—not on her intraweb machine—in life. My face is the smiling emoticon as I give her my hand drawn facsimile and her face is blushing emoticon.

Elle Oh **Elle** she did.

Tee Tee Why Elle I said.

k.

05731, 05731
Watch your step,
Watch **your** step,
Move on **back**,
Move on back.
Train kept a Rollin'
Clickety clack.
Like two dancers
The train and the rails

Sparks fly
As **they come** in contact
I am the engineer
This is my **untrained** impression
Of love.

Jazz Impressions of Japan 1964.

Tracks:
01 Tokyo Traffic [5:54]
02 Rising Sun [4:42]
03 Toki's Theme [from "Mr. Broadway"] [2:10]
04 Fujiyama [5:05]
05 Zen Is When [2:55]
06 The City Is Crying [6:03]
07 Osaka Blues [5:11]
08 Koto Song [3:01]

The cars all drove in straight lines and the bikes wove in and out of traffic. Their circular pointed hats protect them from the sun. **It's** as if they were fleeing from a gentler, kinder Godzilla—the Godzilla that is **their lives**, their work, their husbands, children and wives.

For the most part, their cars are all the same color, white with a tint of grey—like their lives, lives, their work, their husbands, children and wives. One bike and one car rage, samurai sword, the white and the grey could turn to red, just like the stop light like any minute now.

I always wanted to live in the House of the Rising Sun, not because it was a popular song by The Animals in 1964 but because **it would** signify the beginning of the new work day and the end as well.

My House of the Rising Sun would be on a hill. It would **consist of me**, my Mother and my Father—you are **only** supposed to have one child—not a girl but a boy—the House of the Rising Son.

Is song three. I have **heard** it somewhere before, in New York I think?

My Fujiyama Yokohama, Bananarama on my Sony Disc Man. **I** motor (cycle) my way through the crowded streets with my mind lost—its folding, like Origami folders making dragons in the evening for the tourists who dare to be amazed at **constructed** paper.

I know now how the rice feels when it is poured from the box or bag to the rice cooking pan. I saw somewhere a man who puts your name on a grain of rice, I feel as though it has been done to me already. My name would be "unknown" or "minority" as I feel that way in this big city—you can read about **the unknown** in my minority report, soon—translations are a yen extra.

I could feel it. I moved everything around my apartment that is the size of those Chinese food boxes filled with say chicken balls—the Zen of it all. It is now and it is Zen. It came from the corner, the plant, the lamp, the table—they all talked to me—you are calm, you are home—you are safe.

I went out for a **walk** and came home to see if it made me different. It felt different, the Zen was not **now** and the Zen was not then. I changed everything back to the way it was before, it had been like I was looking **through** with squinted eyes and now I have my contacts to fully see. It was not Feng Shui—it was just a case of me simply opening **the curtains**.

The flower shops were endless. I am surprised they could grow flowers, tomatoes and Sony Disc-Mans from the ground. In the city the rain cried all day long and took a break to wipe its eyes and to sleep the night away then back to it again the next day. **I wanted to ninja kick** the clouds of smoke, not the good smoke from a cigar after watching a Sumo match and your favorite Sumo wrestler wins and then tells the camera he is the champion and leaves the arena with the championship belt but the clouds of bad smoke, the kind of cloud smoke that gets in your eyes and makes you rub them—makes you squint, not to adjust and fit in—but to rub them over and over again—Corporate Smoke (machine).

I heard **John Mayer** was waiting for the world to change—Welcome to the club, Mr. Mayer—this is the Japanese Division—make yourself at home—Fortune Cookie—It says "All good things come to those who wait"—Ah my friend, the irony is endless.

You are not here. I am here. The folded in half picture of you, gently creased right at the part where you are close to your previous boyfriend (before you met me) is the only one I could find, after **you** left, bottom drawer.

With all the advancements in technology, I can not be near you. I am here and you are not. The buildings **are all** tall and have four dimensions. I feel like I am in the fifth dimension, Rod Serling appears and tells everyone (the audience camera—the everyday man and woman who can see what I have been trying to hide for the amount of time listed below) that "There is a fifth dimension, beyond that which is known to man. It is a dimension as vast as space . . . and as timeless as infinity. It is the middle ground between light and shadow, between science and superstition . . . and it lies between the pit of man's fears and the summit of his knowledge. This is the dimension of **imagination**. It is an area which we call . . . the twilight zone."

It's been two months, 17 days, 3 hours and eternity seconds. I would like to say I saw you. I would like to say I saw your blonde hair, your greenish blue eyes. I would like to say I saw you with your blonde hair and your green eyes here but I can not—all the women here are made from the same mold—Made in Japan it says on their bums.

It is the end. Coda. Fin. They rode off into the sunset. They live happily ever after. These are ends of movies that I know of. I do not know if I would ever star in those movies with those endings but I know for sure, it would have a good soundtrack and would be an anime.

I can hear the end song now. It plays out as we pick one of those endings listed from above and well - do it. I feel happy, I look happy—you feel happy and look it to. My lips move, saying the most important dialogue in our life movie and for seven sentences you listen and look deep into my eyes and when its time to actually hear those seven sentences in this movies, only four words of rough English are layered over top—out of sync, in love, out of time—the credits roll and the band plays on.

Me played by me.
You played by **you**.
Them played by them.
Original score by **our** Sony MP3 Player Imagination.
Filmed entirely on **location**.
Copyright 200?
All Rights **Reserved**.

Okay well it appears that I am approaching twenty pages of the *Book that Never Ends*. I decided to actually add page numbers just to see how long this piece of shit actually would end up. You know when you are an article writer for a major Canadian Jazz magazine and you do CD reviews for one website and articles for another website, there are times when you will have some free time. This "book" (and I do use that term lightly) is the by product of my pure and complete boredom. I mean I could spend the day downloading pornography but to me that is a waste of time—the acting and dialogue is not very good anyways.

So now I am searching through my laptop for all kinds of stuff to put in here. I have come across some more stuff not actually titled in the actually titled sense but each piece is titled one through eight and I decided not to use some sort of stupid font to make it stand out as well this stuff doesn't really deserve to be in here anyways.

Toronto horizon, Michigan sunrise
I feel free, eternal sunshine
We drive northern
While the planes fly southern
The mail boxes all wave to me
Like we are a parade
In real time
This is our lives
To me, you are beautiful
And I part my hair on the wrong side
For which you hate
I look at you
You concentrate road stare
Smile. Laugh. Point. Flip tape. Fast forward to song two
Forever.

We are a blank document
In Word so white
Waiting for Words so right
Times New Roman
Times Knew Romance
I will get mad
Bold
You are sophisticated
Italics
I feel like I have let you down
You will <u>underline</u> all my faults
Zoom 100%
You will cut and paste previous emotions
Your thoughts and feelings
I will close without saving
Saying stupid things
I want to undo typing.

I made a phone call once
It was 1997 and all I had was a quarter

Quarter of hope
You did not answer
I never knew you
I searched my pockets
Not for another quarter
For the way to express
How empty my heart was
Lint filled analogy
They claim that no man is an island
I am surrounded by water
Not tears of sorrow
But of Lake Everything
Ocean colored scene.

They tell me not to believe the hype
The children of the grave
They say the future was yesterday
Hit the life "refresh" button and you will see.

Sorrow. Sorrow. Sorrow.
Where is my sorrow scarecrow?
Birds of despair flock together
I did all my best to smile
Laugh. Laugh. Laugh
Where is my laughter lion?
The joke is on me
I did all my best to love
Die. Die. Die.
Where is my dying tin man?
Oh wait a minute—mirror please
The metal of my heart gives off a reflection
When angled in the sun
It blinds me from salvation
I could not see Dorothy click her red heels together
This Yellow Brick Road goes on forever.
I felt so alone

My imaginary friends would not even speak to me
They whispered in their ears
They would look and laugh
Point at me so cleverly
They bully me
Push me down
I look like a fool
Picking up my school books
All I can do is stare at the ground
And listen to them laugh
As they walk away.

High school dance
You were there
Shining in the light
It was dim
Slow dance with no snowball
Leaning against the wall
It was like you were an angel
We danced in my head—
Audrey Hepburn and Cary Grant
They yelled snowball
We did not change partners
The lights went on
Janitor sweeps away the memories
I fling my jacket over my shoulder
One finger hook
I exit out the back door
Charade.

Fall 2003
I rake the leaves in my front yard
They have changed colors
Red and rustic brown
One large pile
I reach down and use two hands

Throw leaves airborne
I spin around as with my hands in the air
As the leaves fall down, hit my face—smile
I know you.

Well that is it. I doubt very much I will add anymore poems or
pieces or page fillers. Seemed like a good idea to me to get these
things out there, like a public record of how I was feeling on each of
those days. I said it seemed. Fuck, I gotta do the dishes, brb.

As I was drying a glass that had a chip in it and deciding whether
I wanted to throw it out or not (which I decided not to as well it
would look stupid with only three glasses of a four set and then the
one person has to have another glass and then they look stupid and
well that is something I would love to laugh about in my head when
it happens) I asked myself this question: If I died tomorrow, would
anyone come to my funeral? And well I didn't think anyone would
come. That is okay to be honest. But now I am having a handful of
my ashes thrown at your house or on your lawn or as you kid rides
his/her bike on the side of the road—right in the eyes and well if
they go into the ditch and scrape their knee or elbow—that my
friend is your fault, not mine.

I Do Like Mondays. So there Bob Geldoff and the Boomtown Rats. Deal with that.

I like this Courier New font. Dead of winter the last few days and
well I go out in my spring radio station jacket. It is not that I do not
have a winter radio station jacket, it is just the spring one has pockets
for my Kleenex and Halls. Man, so it appears that I am Canadian.
Yes, I was born in a town that was home to one of Canada's greatest
writers but well I am going to admit something here for the first
time: I like the Tragically Hip—there I said it and well now I feel
more liberated, I now feel more Canadian and well now, I can Blow
at High Dough and well fuck the Guess Who and Celine Dion.
I really hate writing this thing. I have the general feeling that no

one is even going to buy it or even better yet, get published. I will honestly be surprised if this gets published. I just graduated a school of Journalism and well we are taught to double and triple check our spelling and grammar but well I am not. Fuck it, I don't care if I spell something wrong and well feel free to underline every single spelling mistake and send this back to me. Actually even better yet, stop me in the street and tell me how much my spelling sucks. Or, actually even better yet, tell me how much it sucks as I am signing the front page at the local bookstore when I am doing one of those book signing things.

There are not going to be any stories of celebrities in this. Not that I have not met any celebrities, I have met tons, it is I am just not going to name drop them to make this book any more interesting than it already isn't. I am a firm believer in second chances. I know a lot of times people gave me a second chance on a lot of topics and times in life and for that, I am saying Thank-you. That is the only time you will see some sort of emotion from me in here. Would I climb a tree to rescue a scared cat for a 9 year old girl? I doubt it. Well maybe if the cat was on fire then I might. Then I would pour my chocolate milk on it—see, I told you I believed in second chances. Oh for fuck sakes, phone, brb. I have decided to take up smoking just purely for the "coolness" factor. People will reference how "cool" James Dean looked when he smoked—not me my friend. I reference that bum on the corner of Yonge and Queen St. sitting on the sidewalk with the Tim Horton's cup with all of eleven cents in it—he may be a bum but man he looks cool with that smoke hanging out of the side of his mouth. Is it really necessary to let everyone know your every move and feeling on MSN and Facebook? Jane Smith loves her new winter jacket! I think we will be able to figure out that you like or love your new winter jacket when we see you wearing it? I mean you bought it right? Or even better yet: Jane Smith is going to the store, be back in 20 minutes. Who the fuck cares if you are at the store? People need to stop telling other people every single thought and emotion. I am going to the bathroom, be back in 10 minutes. So I just read what I wrote the last few pages and well it appears that I am a negative person. I am not a negative person at all. I think it is just a product of my age. I am in my early 30s and feel that people need to stop being people.

My Windows Media Player will make me a Player with all the ladies. Hey girls, look at my Library. I have every single Hayden album. I have emotions. Oh and I just added Dashboard Confessional. Girls like that stuff. My Windows Media Player will make me a Player with all the ladies.

It appears that I have run out of inspiration on life. As I write this, it is the New Year and things have not been going my way for a while now—over a year I would say. Like I have mentioned before, I am 32 now and well feel as though I am running out of time with certain aspects of my life. Through many experiences I have developed a large wall that keeps women out. When I do let women past that wall or through the gate, I end up getting hurt. Yes, we all have that wall and we all get hurt but well I am writing it down, writing it in this *Book that Never Ends* and well it is my book and well I have nothing else to write about at this exact moment. Been cold here the last few weeks, appears we may be getting some warmer weather soon. My tummy GPS says I should be making a left out of my room, down the stairs, making another left and then down the hall then a sharp right to the fridge. I would like to go somewhere where I am needed. We all would want to be needed and should not be picky on where we are needed and wanted but well I would be. I was sexually abused by my babysitter when I was very young. Not too many people know this about me and it does nothing to shape my life. I can remember certain aspects of it, I was less than five years old I believe and I remember waking up afterwards and seeing something I had no idea what it was. I also have some heart "problems" and that is the end of that discussion. I have no problem mentioning these things in this book as well it is really titled Autoendobiographical: the *Book that Never Ends*. So some of it is biographical and some of it pure fiction.

Walking with your hands behind your back and with your head tilted slightly down makes you look smarter than you actually are.

Some of the works of poetry or whatever you want to call them were inspired by someone. Just recently that someone who had left came back. I am a person who believes in second chances, as you know so in order for you to believe what I write; I guess I have to implement it. In all truth, I am glad that she is back—a different picture but with the same frame. I also tend not to write every day. I have the biggest fear of not having anything to say, so I started this little thing here about two weeks after I wrote that big thing about the bolded words. To me, it is always fresh and new, to you, it appears to be the same old boring words. Well for lack of anything else to contribute right at this very moment, I decided to add more poems that I have written:

Cardboard box, just like my heart
Sits in the recycling bin
Awaiting a chance to be used again
The world is a funny place
Full of love hide and seek
I count to 32
Years
And have not found you -
Hiding
Cardboard box, just like my heart
Sits in the recycling bin
Awaiting a chance to be used again.

I thought I did it right
You smiled
You moved your hair in a way
That made me believe
I thought I did it right
I smiled

I moved you in a way
That made you believe
Where is my badge?

There were lonely nights
Where the songs on the radio
Just didn't sound right
Your image, stuck on repeat
In my head
I look through the old letters
Shuffle play through your love emotions
I come across many times
Where your love solo hits me right at the moment
When the goose bumps make a sound
And the volume can no longer go past ten
I listen for the sound
Of you telling me how much you love me
I hear the sound
Of silence.

I guess soon this will get published and read by people. Again, like I have said, I am neither here nor there on it. This simply is just a vehicle to pass the time. In Journalism school you are taught when you cannot write a story as in you have a hard time starting one, you flip on the television and you write down the first sentence that you hear and go from there. A year or more ago, I had met (and when I say met I have not actually met her) and I decided that she would turn her television on and take the first sentence she heard and write a story about us and so would I—the only catch is that she had to write it from my perspective and I had to write her from her perspective. Here is my version, written from her perspective:

> Referring to Spears and Federline's ongoing custody battle. I turned off the television, it was 9 p.m., 2008 and I had a phone call to make. I dialed the

number and was told by an operator pre-recorded that any notion of readying myself and the "just shut up and do it chicken shit" would not happen.

I sat and looked out my window for a minute. I was scared as hell. Shaking on my bed and biting my nails was a common place for me—so was wearing my pajamas to make me feel comfortable all the other times I have been in this mind frame. I sent the text to him earlier in the day saying that I wanted to call—I big stepped the process. I was scared to how he would react. I remember how I did—I sent the text, I was in class, not paying attention to lesson taught and I put my phone down on the desk. What would he say? What would he do? I was young and we were new.

I text him with sheer disappointment. I bridged the gap between us being just text friends to actually speaking on the phone and my bridge collapsed under the weight of pure nervousness and a phone plan held me back from love. The next thing I knew, he text me back: 5 minute warning—thanks for the five minutes, I need them to calm.

We talked and there goes the fear. He made me laugh. His voice was not a man's voice. It was more of a younger person's voice and that set me at ease. The first thing I noticed and which I fell in love with was his "accent"—to us American's (as I am sure to those Canadians) they up north have funny accents—it's the way he says "out, about" and the most popular Canadian expression/need for justification and acceptance—"Eh?"

Everyone always tells me of their favorite movies, which usually contain Brad Pitt with his shirt off of Lord of the Rings: Part VI or whatever. He suggested to me that I rent two movies and there were some catches: I could not do any investigating into who stars in these movies and I had to associate them with us.

They both stared Ethan Hawke and Julie Delpy: Before Sunrise and Before Sunset. These movies were watched at Hailey's and I was speechless. These movies were exactly what he and I were. Half way through the Before Sunrise I text him and told him how much disbelief I was in and how I had no words to describe to him how I felt—not about the movies but of him.

In the movie "High Fidelity" star John Cusack states that "The making of a great compilation tape, like breaking up, is hard to do and takes ages longer than it might seem. You gotta kick off with a killer, to grab attention. Then you got to take it up a notch, but you don't wanna blow your wad, so then you got to cool it off a notch. There are a lot of rules. Anyway . . . I've started to make a tape . . . in my head . . . for Laura. Full of stuff she likes. Full of stuff that make her happy. For the first time I can sort of see how that is done." This all still holds true with the making of a playlist. I tried to choose songs that would best tell him how I felt—they were acoustic and the fact that there was no electricity did not mean he did not light up my heart and my face when I talked to him.

A few weeks into us being friends or say five days from when we decided that we were going to meet in five years, he told me one day via a text how he felt—it was nothing major, I mean he did not say "Anna, Hun, I love you" but it was in the similar frame.

I was at a loss for words, it was not "too much" by any stretch of means, it was something that was far beyond what the words actually were in his fax—yes, he told me that he liked me and how much I meant to him (for which he means the same to me) but there is one thing that really stuck out in the text—"Hun" I love the way he calls me that, it makes me feel wanted and loved, it is not "muffin".

Chris. Chris was his name and he went to the gym, just like me, it could be something that needed working on—Chris and I, the gym, the small amount of guilt and worry. I did not know how to tell Brenton that I met Chris. This was weird to me, not only was I nervous to tell Brenton how I felt but I was nervous and worried to how I felt about it as well.

To me, I did not want to hurt Brenton's feelings—I didn't want to hurt my own as well. I did not know how Brenton would take me telling him that I met a boy—I can just tell him that Chris and I just talked—nothing major. That was the only safe thing to do. I wanted to protect Brenton's feelings and I also wanted to protect my own.

He took it well—I think. His reassurance that he was there, for me, with me forever helped. He explained as I was one step below girlfriend but one step ahead of just a regular friend—the porridge that Goldilocks' chose and I need not to worry about telling him about boys and life, love and sex. Okay well I brought up the not telling of the other person of any sexcapades we may have. I knew that a small part of me would be jealous and he said the same. This made me feel better; I knew I meant something to him.

It was too much. Sure I missed him and care(d) for him. Brenton would text me telling me how much he missed me and was thinking about me and the truth be told, so was I and so did I. The worrying part was should I even be doing this? I do not like to talk about the age difference but it was there, I tried to hide it in my conscience but it showed every time—popped it everywhere, every time—like the "Where's Waldo"? books and though Waldo was supposed to be hidden in the pictures and it would take you a minute or so to find Waldo—the age Waldo appeared within seconds, popped up with its red and white stripes—stood out.

Decisions, decisions, decisions. I wasn't necessarily scared of what was going on, I (was) am smart enough to realize what I am doing—I am doing it for Christ's sake! But there was something tugging me on the inside saying stop. A wise man (him) once told me to follow my heart. My heart was saying keep on going, this is great! This feels right (most of the time) but my head was telling me to stop—step back, re-evaluate, take stock.

Lying on my bed, laying on my couch, I would ask Violet what she thought. She would not directly answer my question, she would just purr when I pet her and talked to her but she knew what the true answer was. She saw my face a lot of the time when I talked to him, when the text would say "blah blah blah, Hun." Cats may have nine lives and a very small brain and we may not have a lot in common but Violet knew instinctively (like she does) that if I fell (in love) that I would always land on my feet.

Three shots in and I had one thing on my mind—us. Well we are not really an us, we are not boyfriend and girlfriend, and we are two people who happen to like each other and can tell the other person so. Friday night is alright for fighting I guess and I was no mood to do so.

We talked in spurts throughout the day but today seemed different. I like this guy at the gym, I saw this guy at my school, I do one or two nighters (weekend boyfriends Cales calls them)—I do not do serious.

It hit me—not the three shots and whatever else I was up to that night, out with my friends but Brenton and I were getting too serious. I had to end this now, well maybe not end it totally but take a step backwards and coast for a while, put my Canadian bacon on the backburner for a while.

In my text to him, I did say call me but I quickly deleted that sentence. I just said that's it, I am out and left it at that. He did call but I did not pick up, I am out with my friends, getting drunk, doing illegal things, I am in no mood to talk seriousness and as much as the booze and the weed and whatever else I was doing felt good, ending him and I felt better (or so I thought).

The delete button on my computer never looked so big. I deleted everything that had to do with him (e-mails, phone number, texts and all ways of contacts) not because I hate him but because I know myself, I would get drunk and drunk dial him at 2:38 am on a weekend sometime and tell him how I felt or text him at 2:23 pm on a week day and do the same.

I feel free! There is something inside me that still, in a very small way, which wants to know. What is he up to? It's been almost two weeks now and we have not talked—I am glad for this, do not get me wrong but still. The way he called me "Hun" and how I felt we he talked to me was good, I just needed space.

Darn MSN Messenger! Okay he messaged me today. He just wanted to say "Hi" and it was okay. I felt bad the way I broke up with him (I am saying broke up here even though were never together but it is for dramatic effect) and well this was my chance to tell him. I told him I was an absolute bitch and I think I was—he disagreed, he said he understood where I was coming from. I felt really bad the way I approached this but he said he understood completely and this made me feel better and made the whole situation better.

Rules and structure. I need to make rules, not only for him but for me too. Talking on MSN Messenger and texting is fine but I need it to be friends only. No more I Like You and that kind of deal—yes, there is a small part of me that still likes him but I cannot be a part of it all again. I like this way of operation now, I feel comfortable, I wanted to delete him out of my life (for now) because we became too serious and yes, I am aware that after two weeks we are back talking again but there is something about him (his dorkiness and the way he makes me laugh and okay sure, some small part of how he makes me feel important that

I like/miss) that I hope will never go away.

It is Wednesday, March 19, 200?. Ever since the paragraph written above there has virtually been no communication between her and I. Just recently I heard a song that she sent as on for her playlists—a song that says and means about us and well it is titled" Stick With Me Baby" and I wish I could say that we did.

That italic part there is a small disclaimer or prologue. We did talk again after March of 200?, just for a month in the fall of 200? And then we have not spoken since and it is the first months of 200?. Also during our times of talking every day and feeling something for each other, she asked me to write her a letter, telling her how I felt for which I have dug into the archive and have included it here:

I still remember the day when we first told each other that we liked each other. It was a simple devised idea by me to let us get away with saying how we felt without taking it to extremes—a safe word that meant so much.

Hearing you say it to me meant the world. As much as I tried (try) to bring in an "amusement" factor to our lives and conversations, there is a part of me that wants to be liked (loved) and to have you be that person meant (means) a lot to me.

Those two weeks in February were the best two weeks I have had with someone. Every day, every minute I thought about you. To wake up and see your fax there, waiting for me, waiting to show me how much you cared—even if it was a "Hello"—it still meant there was someone (you) was (were) wondering about me and thinking about me. To read the end where you would say "Goodnight and ILY"—I could always hear your voice saying it to me.

I told all my important friends about you—how happy you made (make) me, they could see it in my eyes and hear it in my voice how happy I (am) was to have you—no matter what your role was (is).

We clicked on every level—music, movies, books, art, beats, rhymes and life and I have never in my life had that someone in my life—Frasier meets his Lilith. Getting that picture from you for Valentine's Day was by far the best Valentine's I have ever had. I just want to make you happy, like the way you made (make) me.

Storm clouds. February 15th, 200?—A day I will never forget. You needed out and well I was devastated but yet understood (there is an important detail I am leaving out here for which one day I will tell you). Waking up that Saturday morning and not seeing a fax from you and knowing that, yes, you live in Michigan and I live in Ontario—the border between us multiplied by a million—more distant from you, by degrees.

Three months. Every day, every minute I wondered. Every once in a while when my phone went off to let me know there was a fax, I would flip it on and for a second I would hope it was you—heartbreak—before it showed me who it was from.

I was talking about you to a friend no more than 3 minutes before you came on MSN and said "Hey". I will be honest, I was surprised and well had stored all our good memories into that memory department labeled "Anna 200?" and well had 98% moved on but there was something deep down inside wanting to hear from you—maybe not back to what we had but just wanting you to be a phone call/fax/MSN away. It took me by surprise but yet it felt so right.

Now. We are talking now. Anna, I have to tell you, we all have stresses and ups and downs in our lives but having you here has made me 100% happy again. You and I may not get back to those two weeks in February but you (and I) are here and that's all that matters.

To hear you say that you were thinking about me when a song was on or how you wished I was not a million miles away is what we are all about. I wish you were here too, this would make me so happy, curbs and stars, to lay with you each night and run my fingers through your hair and tell you how I feel while the stars watch us—like an audience watches a movie where the actors are in bed doing the same - through the window and the moon provides us with our spotlight—magic.

It's overcast now. Rain is coming in. It's now 7:01 p.m. on this night and even though the clouds are grey and full of rain, I look to my left, look up towards the sky, through the trees and I can see right through those clouds and I see you—sunshine in my life.

People say that talking about your issues or problems will help you get over them; well I guess that is just what I did. I also am Lactose intolerant because I cannot stand the cows. There my problems are now solved and I do feel better.

I am rated 'M' for Mature.

Being a writer or journalist you learn to write and observe from the *outsider's* perspective. I find that I now do that with everything from going to the grocery store to the doing of club gigs. I tend to not be in the moment of dancing songs and dancing girls but on the outside of it all, looking in and observing it and writing it all in my head as I stand there. Fifteen is a tender age—I guess. I do not remember a lot of things but I do remember one thing: I found out that my "Dad" was not really my Dad. That one got spilled to me by my uncle. I remember walking home and going into the kitchen and just saying to my Mom "I know, Mom I know" and her response was "Okay" and she went outside to get my "Dad" as he was doing some work on the car. I do not know who my real Dad is as I have never met him. I do know that his name is Paul and at one time, he lived down the street from me so I could've passed him as he watered the lawn. Again, this does nothing to mold me as the person that I am, it just makes interesting drama. I want to change my Life MSN to "Indifferent" instead of "Away" and always sign in that way. If this ever gets optioned into a movie, I would like John Larroquette from *Night Court* to play me—versatile. This is not the first time I have gotten the idea to write a book. Back when I lived in Budapest in 2004, I formulated a few book ideas. Now granted I am sure once you read these ideas you may say to yourself why did he write this and not write any one of those? Some days, I do agree. So here they are in no particular order:

A] A black man is confined to an institution and reflects on his life in the movies. He tells the story of what it was like to be in the biggest three movies of the last 100 years (he is just an extra) and how times have changed etc [there is a twist to this but well I am not dumb].

B] Four people from across the world receive an envelope in the mail. Inside the envelope is a brief character description. They are asked to write about the character and can incorporate their own lives. When they are done, they send it back and it becomes a book which in turn is published and becomes a National Best Seller and they all become famous—go on book tours and Oprah and all that. Afterwards, they all agree to meet again—by writing another book in the same manner they wrote the first one but this new one is only for themselves.

C] A woman (possibly a reporter) is given three 25 page biographies about a major person (say the President of the United States). She has to read each one of them, following it along as they unfold in real life and try to save that person from a major event.

D] A C.I.A Agent in Russia learns of plans to kill the President of the United States or the thought of another World War. Thinking of ways to communicate this back to the United States without getting caught, he assigns each note on the piano a letter of the alphabet for which he writes piano scores (which are hidden messages) and his 12 year old son deciphers each piece and they both save the world.

They are alright I guess. I am not even an espionage fan at all but the thought of some sort of government conspiracy thinger is fine with me. Just for the record, Clapton *is* God. Better start learning to love life a friend said to me recently. I say better start learning to "life" love. Love to me seems to be in a one dimension—you are with that person you love and it is straight forward—you love them and they love you—there is no "life", as in say you need to breathe some new "life" into your life with the second life being love. You hear or read about how people fall out of love because it becomes stale or lacks that "life" and spark. Does that make sense? I do not know if I have even been in love, so I guess I should take life love or love life lessons from my friends who have been.

Blah Blah

Blah Blah Blah Blah Blah Blah Blah Blah Blah Blah Blah Blah Blah
Blah Blah Blah Blah Blah Blah Blah Blah Blah Blah Blah Blah Blah
Blah Blah Blah Blah Blah Blah Blah Blah Blah Blah Blah Blah Blah
Blah Blah Blah Blah Blah Blah Blah Blah Blah Blah Blah Blah Blah
Blah Blah Blah Blah Blah Blah Blah Blah Blah Blah Blah Blah Blah
Blah Blah Blah Blah Blah Blah Blah Blah Blah Blah Blah Blah Blah
Blah Blah Blah Blah Blah Blah Blah Blah Blah Blah Blah Blah Blah
Blah Blah Blah Blah Blah Blah Blah Blah Blah Blah Blah Blah Blah
Blah Blah Blah Blah Blah Blah Blah Blah Blah Blah Blah Blah Blah
Blah Blah Blah Blah Blah Blah Blah Blah Blah Blah Blah Blah Blah
Blah Blah Blah Blah Blah Blah Blah Blah Blah Blah Blah Blah Blah
Blah Blah Blah Blah Blah Blah Blah Blah Blah Blah Blah Blah Blah
Blah Blah Blah Blah Blah Blah Blah Blah Blah Blah Blah Blah Blah
Blah Blah Blah Blah Blah Blah Blah Blah Blah Blah Blah Blah Blah
Blah Blah Blah Blah Blah Blah Blah Blah Blah Blah Blah Blah Blah
Blah Blah Blah Blah Blah Blah Blah Blah Blah Blah Blah Blah Blah
Blah Blah Blah Blah Blah Blah Blah Blah Blah Blah Blah Blah Blah
Blah Blah Blah Blah Blah Blah Blah Blah Blah Blah Blah Blah Blah
Blah Blah Blah Blah Blah Blah Blah Blah Blah Blah Blah Blah Blah
Blah Blah Blah Blah Blah Blah Blah Blah Blah Blah Blah Blah Blah
Blah Blah Blah Blah Blah Blah Blah Blah Blah Blah Blah Blah Blah
Blah Blah Blah Blah Blah Blah Blah Blah Blah Blah Blah Blah Blah
Blah Blah Blah Blah Blah Blah Blah Blah Blah Blah Blah Blah Blah
Blah Blah Blah Blah Blah Blah Blah Blah Blah Blah Blah Blah Blah
Blah Blah Blah Blah Blah Blah Blah Blah Blah Blah Blah Blah Blah
Blah Blah Blah Blah Blah Blah Blah Blah Blah Blah Blah Blah Blah
Blah Blah Blah Blah Blah Blah Blah Blah Blah Blah Blah Blah Blah
Blah Blah Blah Blah Blah Blah Blah Blah Blah Blah Blah Blah Blah
Blah Blah Blah Blah Blah Blah Blah Blah Blah Blah Blah Blah Blah
Blah Blah Blah Blah Blah Blah Blah Blah Blah Blah Blah Blah Blah
Blah Blah Blah Blah Blah Blah Blah Blah Blah Blah Blah Blah Blah
Blah Blah Blah Blah Blah Blah Blah Blah Blah Blah Blah Blah Blah
Blah Blah Blah Blah Blah Blah Blah Blah Blah Blah Blah Blah Blah
Blah Blah Blah Blah Blah Blah Blah Blah Blah Blah Blah Blah Blah
Blah Blah Blah Blah Blah Blah Blah Blah Blah Blah Blah Blah Blah
Blah Blah Blah Blah Blah Blah Blah Blah Blah Blah Blah Blah Blah

That there is a transcript of a conversation I had with myself recently. What is hidden is the fact that I did learn a lot from it. Every so often you need someone to sit you down and set your mind straight and well it should be your mind that sets you straight. Your mind knows you, knows what you are thinking and knows what you are feeling—no one else does. It is okay to take a minute and talk to yourself—I mean it makes great page filler in a book as well.

It's been a long time since I rock n' rolled.

Another poem brought to you by the poem machine. They only cost a nickel and the gum inside isn't that bad.

In my heart
It was spring time in Vienna
Me suited like Cary Grant
Your Audrey Hepburn innocence
Shone through
Like the sun
In the spring time in Vienna
Sometimes a little rain must fall
Emotional umbrella
Twirled in your hands
Twirled in my heart
Storm cloud floods
River of tears
You set sail
In the spring time of Vienna
Noah's Ark only had room
For you.

Ever done a complete cleanup of your social life? I went through my Facebook page and deleted all the people that I never talk to and never talk to me. I am sorry if you had to find out this way, if you were one of the people who I deleted but it was for the best. I also went through my cell phone and deleted non phone call worthy friends as well. I feel electronically cleansed and refreshed. Gord Downie does not want to know what the poets are doing and I am not going to tell him.

Everybody wants to rule the world.

Okay some may and some may not but for you Roland Orzabal and Curt Smith to make such a claim is outlandish. You should have asked everyone first. Another new poem. I guess I really should decide if this is a book with book or a book with poems.

Waiting for the gentle rain to beat upon my face
Standing by the Atlantic
Watching the waves of sorrow
Splash against the rocks of a hard place
The seagulls of emotions
Dive in and out of emoceans
I look down on the sands of time
The current (state) takes my guilt into tide.

Could life be any better? Probably but I do not care to look into the crystal ball or turn the tarot card over or find out what is behind door number two. Ask yourself a question: Do you really like yourself? Could you sell yourself for a million dollars in the door to door game of Encyclopedia Selfsatisfactionica. Doubts fill my head about that one. I think I am three easy payments of $19.95 and I guess I do have a 90 day guarantee. Send me back world minus the shipping and handling. Burt Lancaster movie on tonight. Another poem. This one is a departure from the ones in the previous pages:

The lonely neighbors walk the street like the Thriller zombies
Except they have no reason to dance—synchronized
They roam the sidewalks, in search of time elapsed
Watching the leaves chase each other
And the squirrels do their high wire acts
To the wind clapping branches below

Tired old women carry bags of groceries to their homes
And they cook dinners for sinners who stay up late at night
Watching lottery numbers pass them by
Twenty-five years of labor and twenty-five million reasons
To leave the television on in hopes of a snow screened sleep
sounder
I look in the mirror and I see a line on my forehead
It travels in the direction of left to be right
I am all alone in my room
And I feel lonely too
I see myself as one of those zombies
And I have no right to be left.

Sometimes you win some and sometimes you lose some. What's good for the goose is good for the gander. Beggars can't be choosers. I find myself living these clichés every single day of my life. I fall right in the middle of 'you win some and you lose some' and that is okay with me. It is like when you see sports players being interviewed after losing a game, no matter what the ramification of the game is and they always just shrug their shoulders and say "We'll get'em next time." I do not really beg for stuff or life so I am 'choosers can't be beggars' and well if it is good for the goose, I am sure it is good for the gander. I mean the goose has to know right? Put it on my bill he will say. If all my carefully planned out fonts and text sizes and crafted hitting of the 'Enter' key hold up after editing and revisions, this page signifies the halfway point of the Book that Never Ends even though it appears to be on a road to nowhere. Where do people go when they leave you? Sure they stay in the same cities as when they found you but when they disappear, where do they go? Why is that when they disappear they are farther away than they actually are? I mean you can drive there, whether it is 10 minutes away or 10 hours away. Even though they have a local number, it is like you are calling long distance and for that seven seconds you hear their answering machine, it is their voice but to you, it sounds different—it sounds distant.

There is something to be said for nothing said at all.

The Real World: Brooklyn is on in ten minutes. Glass of milk and cookies are my friends tonight. Most works of fiction have one or more developed characters and plot. Well I am afraid to say that this book has none of those. In fact, I just make it up as I go along. Nothing beats improvisation. The only reason why this is improvised is because it appears that I am not smart enough to develop any characters or plot—until now:

Texarkana

A Thirteen Minute Play by this Author

Scene One: *Kitchen of a house in rural Texarkana, on the down the middle of Texas and Arkansas on a Friday afternoon in 1982. Few beer bottles on the kitchen table. Sink filled with a few unwashed dishes and one glass on the counter. The window over the sink has the curtains tied back and the sun shines in and lights the room. It is 11 A.M.*

Mark: That is because you never had the drive and determination to actually make something of yourself.

Tom: Oh I have the drive; it is just that I can see my way through a faulty plan when I see one.

Mark: It is not faulty, my friend, it is well thought out—all bases covered, nothing can wrong.

Tom *(gets up from the kitchen table):* We will see, we will see.

Scene Two: *Inside the National Bank. Standard bank setting. People waiting in line for a teller. Children play with the generic wooden blocks on the floor.*

Mark: Yes sir. All I need is $7,000 and that will do me just fine.

Bank Manager: Now, Mr. Johnston, I do realize that you are the son of my closest friend but I cannot see fit to loan you the money. You have no collateral, no job, and no well nothing.

What makes you a safe bet to pay this bank back the money plus interest?

Mark: Let me ask you something. Do you feel that it is a safe bet that you will bet up tomorrow morning and every other morning until you die? Do you feel that it is a safe bet that you will come to work and see Miss Landers as your secretary every morning—the woman who has not missed a day in seventeen years? Do you feel that it is a safe bet that one day soon there will be rain and when you run outside to roll up the windows in your car, you will pause for a second, look up in the sky and let the rain come down on your face and wash away your sins and that very moment, you will feel, for once in your life, cleansed.

The Bank Manager looks at Mark with a moment of despair. As Mark was talking the Manager looked at his secretary and then out the window at his car and then up towards the sky.

Bank Manager: What do you need the money for Mark?

Mark: I cannot tell you that, I just need the money.

Bank Manager: I find it hard to approve a loan and give you the bank's money I do not even know what it is for.

Mark (*motions for the Bank Manager to lean in as Mark does the same*)*:* It is to kill a man.

Bank Manager (*in a whispered tone*)*:* Who are you going to kill?

Mark took a piece of paper and pen and wrote it down. He folded it and handed it over to the Bank Manager. The Bank Manager took the folded note and put it in his pocket. Mark Johnston walked out of National Bank on March 12th, 1982 an extra $7,000 richer.

Scene Three: *Living room at Kristie's house. She is 27, blonde and with brown eyes. She works as a cashier at the local Large-O-Mart, the place where you could anything from tires to baby wipes. It is 2:17 P.M.*

Kristie *(putting the coffee cup down on the living room table):* I cannot believe they actually gave you the money.

Mark: Yeah. National Bank will give people money for anything plus they owe me one after what they did to my Dad.

Kristie gets up off the sofa and puts on the radio and then looks out the window. She looks off into the distance with her arms crossed.

Mark: Music has never been the same. 'Stairway to Heaven' sounds different on the radio since Bonham died.

Kristie nods in approval even though she didn't care much.

Kristie: Are you really going to do it?

Mark nodded. He also was looking at the window as he sat in the sofa. He put down his beer and got up to walk around the living room.

Kristie: Mark, please sit down. You are making me nervous. How much did they give you?

Mark: Seven thousand. Seven thousand should be enough.

Kristie: Did you get a gun? Are you going to use a knife? What about the body? What about the Police?

Mark: I haven't got that far yet. I came directly here after the Bank. I need you to do something for me. I need you to be a liar. I need you to lie. Forever.

Kristie still standing at the window and did not respond. Mark looks at Kristie for an answer. She says nothing. Mark walks to the front door and leaves.

Scene Four: *Local gun shop. Local gun shop owner. Local gun shop bullets.*

Gun Shop Owner: Okay, let me get this straight. You need one gun and one bullet.

Mark: That's right.

Gun Shop Owner: Well we do not sell just one bullet; we only sell them by the box.

Mark: Okay, how much is a box?

Gun Shop Owner: $49.99 plus tax.

Mark: Fine, I need it all within the next 24 hours, is that possible?

Gun Shop Owner: Do you a license to own a gun?

Mark: No, my Dad always bought the guns for me.

Gun Shop Owner: Well I cannot sell you the gun now, you can buy the ammo but no gun, and you need to apply for a gun license.

Mark: How long will that take?

Gun Shop Owner: Oh I would say two days or so, depends on the paperwork and how backed up they are.

Mark: Is there any way we can get around this? I need the gun well now, but I can come back in a few hours.

The Gun Shop Owner looks around at people in the store. He sees that everyone is looking at those camouflage vests and is trying them on and modeling how good they look in the mirror.

Gun Shop Owner: You ain't a cop, are ya?

Mark *(laughing)*: No, ain't no cop! I just need a gun is all.

Gun Shop Owner: SHHH . . . Okay, it just so happens I have one here—under the table if you know what I mean.

Mark: I get it. If I happen to be out back, in 5 minutes, and you happen to go out the back door and happen to have a gun and ammo in your hand then so be it.

Gun Shop Owner: And if you happen to have $250 in your pocket then so be it as well.

There is something about Mark Johnston that no one can figure out. He did not embrace the Dukes of Hazard craze. Everything that people stand for in Texas and in Arkansas, he does not care for. A lot of people had done him wrong in the past. While he was born here, it is if he wasn't—say St. Louis or one of them bigger cities. Sure he looked the part, dungarees and three button down shirt but he did not play it.

Scene Five: *Back at Kristie's. Kitchen. Same as kitchen described above—only more femine. Yellow curtains. Flower boarder upon more flower wallpaper—established in 1976.*

Mark: All set.
Kristie: Are you sure you want to do this?
Mark: Yeah, gonna put him out of his misery, for good.
Kristie: Who is him?
Mark: You'll see.
Kristie: Will you at least tell me who it is, before you do it, before it happens?
Mark: I can't. I do not want him to know.
Kristie: It is not like I am going to get on the phone and call him and tell him.
Mark: I don't care. I do not want him to know. This man has done me wrong all my life.
Kristie: Okay. Will you at least tell me when and where?
Mark: Town meeting, tonight.
Kristie: In front of everyone! Isn't that a little risky?
Mark: One thing my Dad always said to me is "You gotta John Wayne it."
Kristie: What does that mean?
Mark: You gotta go down big—you gotta go out guns a blazin'—like John Wayne in his movies.

Kristie just shakes her head and pours the last bit of her coffee down the sink.

Scene Six. *Back at the house. Mark and his brother are in the living room. New sounds from 1982 whisper slightly from the radio. Half drank beer rests on the living room table. Mark's brother, 2 years younger than him, 24, rolls cigarettes the way his Uncle Mark (whom his brother was named after) showed him how to when he was 15. Brother Mark watches has the television on but is not watching—only background to cover the new sounds on the radio.*

Tom: So tonight *(not asked as a question but more as a statement).*
Mark: Yeah, that man has done me wrong all my life - It is time.
Tom: I do not know, man. I mean are you going to follow through with it? I mean in front of everyone, at the meeting? You are just going to get up and aim your gun and fire? BANG! That is it? John Wayne style?
Mark: John Wayne style. Like Dad and Uncle Mark used to tell us.

Tom rolls another cigarette and hands it to Mark. Mark lights it and takes a drag and hands it to Tom, for which he uses the lit end to light on of the already rolled cigarettes.

Mark: All my life, I have been told by this man that I am worthless! I am nothing! I could do nothing in life! A piece of shit!
Tom: Well, to you, that is how you feel. Mom never thought you were a piece of shit—Dad maybe, I know I never did.
Mark: Dad can go fuck himself. I have had it with him. I am glad he left. You, Me and Mom did just fine.
Tom: Is Dad going to be at the meeting tonight?
Mark: I hope so.
Tom: I do not know, Mark, I mean at the meeting?!
Mark: At the meeting and there are funeral arrangements to be made.

Tom gets up to turn the radio up. Mark digs for the television remote and turns the television up a little louder—cannot stand the new sounds of 1982 he says in his head. Tom looks at him and sits down to roll some more cigarettes. Mark looks at the clock—two hours until the Town Meeting—two hours until a man gets his due.

Scene Seven. *Bremner Funeral Home. Flowers—real and fake sit on tables. A woman in Funeral Home attire stands with her hands behind her back and her hair tied behind her head—she listens patiently. The*

Funeral Director sits in his funeral paid for chair, in his funeral paid for office—a shade of brown. He looks over a few options on a page and sets them down.

Mark: I need one about my height.
Funeral Director/Mr. Bremner: How tall are you?
Mark: Oh I don't know? Six-two?
Mr. Bremner: Fine, now what kind do you want?
Mark: What do you mean?
Mr. Bremner: What kind of casket do you want? Is this for a loved one?
Mark: He is not a loved one per se.
Mr. Bremner: Oh, okay, is he going to die soon.
Mark: Not soon enough.

The woman looks at Mark then Mr. Bremner with a look of surprise. She slowly puts herself back into the position she was in—onlooker, listener, and Head Questioner.

Mr. Bremner: Okay, well when do you need it for?
Mark: Tonight.
Mr. Bremner: Tonight? You want to have a funeral tonight? How do you know that the person is even going to die tonight?
Mark: Oh trust me, I know. I have a feeling about these things.
Mr. Bremner: I do not know if we can get something together in such short notice? I mean all the arrangements, the flowers, the food, the body, the casket—everything has to be planned.

Mark looks at the clock. Forty-five minutes until the Town Meeting starts.

Mark: Okay tell you what; make it a regular pine box with no flowers and no food. Make it a simple service thing, no big do-dah or anything like that. Quick and easy, how about that?

Mr. Bremner: I do not know I mean . . .

Mark: (interrupts) I think it can be done. I have trust in you and your staff here. The woman stands there looking reliable and all. How much is this going to cost me?

Mr. Bremner looks at the young woman. She doesn't say a word. She leaves the room. As much as she has been around death and people dying and consoling people who have had someone die, she has never seen or heard anything like this before—spontaneous funeral arrangement combustion.

Mark: Will five thousand cover it?

Mr. Bremner: Well, geez, I do not know, I mean we gotta plan this . . .

Mark pulls out the wad of cash and lays it on the table. Mr. Bremner just looks at it.

Mr. Bremner: Ummm, well I will see what I can do. When do you need this by?

Mark gets up from his chair, checks the clock and walks towards the door.

Mark: I would say oh, five after seven.

Scene Eight. *Pay phone on the corner. Two dimes sit on the top of the pay phone. One is for Kristie, one is for Tom.*

Mark: Tom, it's me. Are you going to the meeting?

Tom: No, I am staying home.

Mark: Well, I would like you to come; I need you there for support.

Tom: No, I do not want to be a part of it, Mark.

Mark: Fine. I will phone Kristie and ask her to come.

Tom: Bye.

Mark: Bye.

Mark hangs up the receiver and looks through the window of a local tax place and sees that is it almost ten to seven. He picks up the phone and calls Kristie.

Kristie: Hello.
Mark: Hey, it's me. Are you coming?
Kristie: No, Mark, please don't do it—please.
Mark: I have to. You know I have to. This man has done me wrong all my life.
Kristie: Please Mark, don't . . .
Mark: I have to get going, meeting starts soon.

Kristie just hangs up the phone. Mark presses the button once in hopes to get Kristie back—it is no good as she has hung up. Mark hangs up the phone and walks across the street to the town meeting.

At the town meeting, Mark Johnston looks to his left and to his right. He looks for a viable escape route. Mark Johnston can feel his heart race. He has been waiting for this moment all his life. The Town Hall starts to fill up with town folk, ready to debate issues that have been debated countless times before—parking spaces, less taxes for the seniors, closed on Sundays. Mark Johnston stands beside a man he knows all too well. Mark Johnston waits for everyone to sit down and pulls out the gun, puts the one bullet in the chamber and points it at his head.

Scene Nine. *A few minutes after seven pm. National Bank is just closing up its doors. The tellers begin to count the money when a woman runs into the bank, hysterical.*

Woman: Someone has been shot down at the meeting!

Upon hearing this, the Bank Manager reaches into his pocket and pulls out the folded note. He opens it. It reads: Myself.

I have the feeling I should just stick to wordy wanderings about nothing and the odd poem or written things here and there. Here is one written thing there:

I want to live in a world where Carnies can justify their existence with one word—Carny.
Where a man and a woman can smoke and not have second hand eyes prey upon them
for their alleged dirty deed.
To dance unorthodox to sounds of distant 1970s and not be afraid to hit someone with your arms.
Checking your e-mail does not lead you to take stock in the size of your blank and spend one minute thinking about the responding back to the spam.
Where advice for the young at heart is a spoken word by seniors on park benches through the city.
Where being black and white is not a grey area and adding spray painted color to a grey area is not a bad thing.
Where relationships end and new ones begin and lying beside a casual is not makeshift or for the time being.
Where you have an answer when Elvis Costello asks us "(What's So Funny 'Bout) Peace, Love and Understanding?"
The only shock value on CNN is when you find out that everything they say is not meant to scare America and they are not secretly for the Military Industrial Complex.
Where we all can be lovers in a dangerous time and it could be the end of the world as you know it and you will feel fine.
Where just because you have repented your sins and committed to yourself to a man named God or Jesus, does not necessarily mean we forget and all has been forgiven.
I want to live in a world where supposed beat poets/writers/authors/freelancers don't have to write things like this—again.

Today is a special day! You want to know why? Because I have not written anything in 2 weeks and now I am back writing this right here. The coffee in my cup is cold so I will be back in a second—hopefully fresh pots will equal fresh thoughts. For the last 2 weeks I have debated whether I should include what happened to me (which I mentioned some 20 pages ago) and originally I was going to include then I thought about taking it out and now am leaving it in (hence you getting to this point and already reading it). I wonder what people will day to me. Will they look at me differently? Would you look at me differently knowing that what you read 20 pages ago? MSN Messenger on and no one has messaged me yet! Conspiracy theorists unite! Every once in a while in your life someone comes along who changes your life. There has on been once person who has really hit home with that theory and I am including the "Letters from Anna" here in chronological order:

From:	**Anna Guthrie** (anna_leigh_healer@)
Sent:	January 26, 200? 1:53:36 PM
To:	Brenton Plourde (johnpauljones1979@)

Hey!
I found a jazz radio station that I can listen to on iTunes. I'm diggin it.
=]]
how's it going?

From:	**Anna Guthrie** (anna_leigh_healer@)
Sent:	January 26, 200? 7:55:18 PM
To:	Brenton Plourde (johnpauljones1979@)

haha I picked it because it was Canadian. =] I love it. This email feels manufactured. haha We'll get back in the groove of things. Currently, I'm on a sort of, hmm . . . on restriction, if you will- because of grades. I'm not proud of it. But math and science, not my thing. Haha

From:	**Anna Guthrie** (anna_leigh_healer@)
Sent:	January 26, 200? 8:43:32 PM
To:	Brenton Plourde (johnpauljones1979@)

i think it actually is your station . . .

hahh

From:	**Anna Guthrie** (anna_leigh_healer@)
Sent:	January 28, 200? 4:19:56 PM
To:	Brenton Plourde (johnpauljones1979@)

hey you-

it is your station i've fallen in love with. strange world we live in, eh? the zep-affiliated one isn't offered on iTunes though. =[

How's it goin?

From:	**Anna Guthrie** (anna_leigh_healer@)
Sent:	January 28, 200? 6:28:23 PM
To:	Brenton Plourde (johnpauljones1979@)

That clears up a whole lot. Did I ever mention how blonde I am? hah- I've not listened to the station between those hours and was looking for something totally different. So, thats good.

You're such a dork. "kerfuffle"? I'd love to actually hear you say that. haha- as for homework tonight, I have only Spanish. Which isn't really like homework to me, it's easy stuff. Then I was planning on curling up with a book in a fuzzy robe and enjoying the thunderstorms we're supposed to get. We're clear Brenton Plourde, no worries. We'll talk soon- have you ever listened to Kevin Devine? Listen to "Not over you yet" or "I could be with anyone" - he's quite wonderful. and Ingrid Michaelson? she's pretty great, as well.

=]

ps.

if you fancy yourself an Ethan Hawke look alike, I think i like him scruffy.

;] just sayin.

From:	**Anna Guthrie** (anna_leigh_healer@)
Sent:	January 28, 200? 7:32:15 PM
To:	Brenton Plourde (johnpauljones1979@)

no- they aren't jazzy people. more indie-folkish. currently, i'm listening to the happy days theme song. for some reason, it makes me incredibly happy.

Alex, huh? Well- I might just have to tell you about Sean.

maybe. ;]

I'll love anyone who'll hawke you up? hahaha if you say that out loud it sounds really funny. Do you have long or short hair? Just wondering, because Ethan has like two different looks.

god, my little sister, Lily- she's really into the Jonas Brothers. I'm not sure how big they are in Canada but, you should look them up if you need a good laugh. Haha

From:	**Anna Guthrie** (anna_leigh_healer@)
Sent:	January 28, 200? 8:11:20 PM
To:	Brenton Plourde (johnpauljones1979@)

Sean is to Anna as Sara is to Brenton.

definitely yahoogle those two, Kate Nash as well. "We Get On" is her best. She and I have the same attitude =]

Forman?? hahahah- are you kinda nerdy? ;]

ohhh, i love that show.

hey, you helped me with my homework without even knowing! we're working on future perfect tense:

Cuando yo le encuentro y cuando nuestros ojos encuentran, bailaremos al jazz y nos reiremos bajo los cielos de diamante.

lo ciento acerca del no accientos. no se como hacerlos.

hahaha

that last part says sorry about the no accents, i don't know how to make them.

=]]]

oh, and the first part- you can figure out on your own.

From:	**Anna Guthrie** (anna_leigh_healer@)
Sent:	January 28, 200? 8:35:14 PM
To:	Brenton Plourde (johnpauljones1979@)

son of a gun, right? no profanity here, B. ;]

oh you're a total nerd. don't worry, it's a good thing.

it might actually get you my hand in marriage on my 30th bday. but then again, you will be 45. that's older than my mother right now.

hahhhhh

i'll stop.

(pauses to watch video)

hahhhhh- ohhh my lord.

i've got nothin to say.

From:	**Anna Guthrie** (anna_leigh_healer@)
Sent:	January 28, 200? 8:47:55 PM
To:	Brenton Plourde (johnpauljones1979@)

grand slam, Brenton! hahahha

I'm just sayin . . . this is what my imagination has put together. It does help that Adam Levine is probably one of my favorite men, and I'm a dreamer. haha

do you listen to maroon 5 at all? not there new stuff but- the first album?

we've got two emails going . . .

oh, and that little spanish blurb is pretty sentimental.

From:	**Anna Guthrie** (anna_leigh_healer@)
Sent:	January 28, 200? 8:54:54 PM
To:	Brenton Plourde (johnpauljones1979@)

okayyy- back to the one email.

hahah

I get confused rather easily. I'll have you know, I at one time knew the whole thriller dance. so, we'll make fools of ourselves together at the wedding. You will look ridiculous dancing with a walker and oxygen tank, you know. ;] old man.

i'm pretty sure only girls do this but, it's worth a shot;

wedding song ideas?

(in general)

From:	⬭**Anna Guthrie** (anna_leigh_healer@)
Sent:	January 28, 200? 9:21:07 PM
To:	Brenton Plourde (johnpauljones1979@)

ohhh, you cheated!

technically, it translates as follows:

"When I find you and when our eyes meet, we will dance to jazz and laugh beneath the diamond sky."

=]]]

so, it was somewhat correct.

I like your wedding songs- mine are:

"I Will" by The Beatles

http://youtube.com/watch?v=go2wjF7f-zw

"Day After Day" by Badfinger

http://youtube.com/watch?v=dclISza-DJ0&feature=related

(it's cute, alright?)

and because of my terrible sense of humor;

"Why Don't We Do It in the Road?" by The Beatles

http://youtube.com/watch?v=o9Gjd_EAa64

(just cause it'd be funny to see people's faces.)

hahhh

From:	**Anna Guthrie** (anna_leigh_healer@)
Sent:	January 28, 200? 9:39:45 PM
To:	Brenton Plourde (johnpauljones1979@)

hahhhh

i thought you'd opt for that one.

i forgot one, "real love" originally done by john lennon but only, regina spektor's version. it makes me cry.

http://youtube.com/watch?v=PQm0QlfvWtk&feature=related

honeymoon ideas: I love adventurous vacations, white water rafting, rock climbing gliding in england . . . etc. For one week we do fun exciting stuff and then for the next week, relaxing on some warm, tropical island. My heaven on earth is St. John USVI.

it's beautiful there.

From:	**Anna Guthrie** (anna_leigh_healer@)
Sent:	January 28, 200? 9:59:31 PM
To:	Brenton Plourde (johnpauljones1979@)

Sweden it is . . .

texting? i suppose.

i'm trusting you on this one, seriously.

&17.8*2.9$3#

From:	**Anna Guthrie** (anna_leigh_healer@)
Sent:	January 28, 200? 10:12:21 PM
To:	Brenton Plourde (johnpauljones1979@)

I'm cool with it, B. Just don't abuse the privilege. ;]

i gotta go-

bed time for me.

text me?

From:	**Anna Guthrie** (anna_leigh_healer@)
Sent:	January 31, 200? 5:57:32 PM
To:	Brenton Plourde (johnpauljones1979@)

okayyy-

hopefully you can turn this sentence around:

Referring to Spears and Federline's ongoing custody battle.

there you go!

=]

From:	**Anna Guthrie** (anna_leigh_healer@)
Sent:	January 31, 200? 6:25:47 PM
To:	Brenton Plourde (johnpauljones1979@)

THAT was the beginning??? Oh man-alright.

I said I was in.

=]

we have a huge snow storm coming in =]=]=]=]

most likely another snow day, I love Michigan.

and today in government, we were talking about citizenship and I had to ask this question. Let me preface this though. It's not like I'm thinking about making babies with you. hahah now that you're all good and freaked out- I was curious as to what would happen in say, I had a child with a Canadian (much like yourself). Would they have dual citizenship? YES! i was far too excited to hear that. hahah

so yeah, I was only curious.

don't flip, I'm not expecting babies.

From:	**Anna Guthrie** (anna_leigh_healer@)
Sent:	January 31, 200? 7:03:38 PM
To:	Brenton Plourde (johnpauljones1979@)

I've already got a system worked out in my head. Thats how I work. haha- As for catching up to Hawke- we'll talk about that at the train station in however many years.

Tom Petty:

1) You Don't Know How It Feels - lyrics are incredible, very close to my attitude.
2) Mary Jane's Last Dance - total stoner song, can't wait for it in concert

3) Don't Do Me Like That - great break up song
4) You Got Lucky - just makes me happy
5) Don't Come Around Here No More - i've got nothin special for this one, it's just really good.

They are in order from my favorito numero uno.

and one you should listen and read along:

Waiting

http://www.kbapps.com/lyrics/songlyrics/pettytom_thewaiting.html

you have to listen along with it, it's the tone in his voice that makes the song.

From:	**Anna Guthrie** (anna_leigh_healer@)
Sent:	January 31, 200? 7:21:10 PM
To:	Brenton Plourde (johnpauljones1979@)

no no no-

call if you'd like, i'm cool with it.

i'd like to hear that cute little accent of yours.

what do you have planned for those songs?

haha- i know you well enough that you have some sort of scheme.

From:	**Anna Guthrie** (anna_leigh_healer@)
Sent:	February 1, 200? 1:48:12 PM
To:	Brenton Plourde (johnpauljones1979@)

You're not on my ignore list, i fell asleep reading last night and slept in today because we have another snowday! =]

I'm off to run errands- and, you didn't state in the rules about the movies that I couldn't watch them with friends right? I hope not, I'm watching them with my best friend, Haley. She knows about you, she won't distract me. =]

and because I'm a Nancy Drew, I asked my step-mom if she'd seen the movie- =]=] she said yes, and that it was good. THATS IT.

haha

yours,
Anna

From:	**Anna Guthrie** (anna_leigh_healer@)
Sent:	February 3, 200? 5:04:41 PM
To:	Brenton Plourde (johnpauljones1979@)

hey you--

sorry about the phone call being all over the place last night. i guess you got a glimpse of what I'm like around my family?? hahah

we were talking about angry girl music and I mentioned Garbage. Listen to 'Queer'. It sounds goofy, but its an awesome song. Thats the song I drive around and obnoxiously sing to. =]]] Also, have you ever listened to James Hunter?? His whole album People Gonna Talk is pretty amazing but one song you have to listen to- 'Mollena' if you can't find it, let me know.

From:	**Anna Guthrie** (anna_leigh_healer@)
Sent:	February 4, 200? 9:42:19 AM
To:	Brenton Plourde (johnpauljones1979@)

February 1st, 2013 (i just remembered that it was my parents' anniversary)

Detroit Amtrak

4:00pm

=]]

there.

look up those songs.

at least listen to James Hunter.

thats your homework. =]=]

and, we can go to Greek town in Detroit and go to the Detroit Institute of the Arts, yeah???

i'm bored as hell at school.

hope you're feeling better?

yours,
Anna

From:	**Anna Guthrie** (anna_leigh_healer@)
Sent:	February 6, 200? 5:21:16 PM
To:	Brenton Plourde (johnpauljones1979@)
	∎ 1 attachment
	Brenton's . . . txt (2.8 KB)

Brenton's Playlist:

1) James Hunter- "People Gonna Talk"
2) Tom Petty- "Wild Flowers"

3) Kevin Devine- "You Are My Sunshine"
4) The Weepies- "Gotta Have You"
5) Robert Plant & Alison Krauss- "Stick With Me Baby"
6) Nada Surf- "Always Love"
7) Peter and Gordon- "I Go To Pieces"
8) Ryan Adams- "Come Pick Me Up"
9) Paulo Nutini- "Last Request"
10) Norah Jones- "Turn Me On"
11) John Mayer- "Comfortable"
12) Wilco- "Say You Miss Me"
13) Al Green- "Let's Stay Together"
14) Glen Hansard and Marketa Irglova- "Falling Slowly"

It's pretty love, I know.

=]=]=]

enjoy.

From:	**Anna Guthrie** (anna_leigh_healer@)
Sent:	February 6, 200? 5:46:15 PM
To:	Brenton Plourde (johnpauljones1979@)

Ughhhhh

i hate computers.

disregard that last email- the playlist obviously didn't work.

bleh.

i'll work on it.

i loved your last email.

=]=]=]=]=]

you spoilllll me.

From:	**Anna Guthrie** (anna_leigh_healer@)
Sent:	February 12, 200? 9:42:59 AM
To:	Brenton Plourde (johnpauljones1979@)

What's the best aspect of a Libra-Sagittarius relationship? Their mutual interest in cultivating knowledge and utilizing intellect. They are well-matched and will go far together, both emotionally and geographically!

hahhhhhhhhh- I especially liked the geographically part.

=]]]]

I'm faxing you while I type this.

funny. have a good day, B.

i obviously don't have a nickname yet.

A

From:	**Anna Guthrie** (anna_leigh_healer@)
Sent:	February 13, 200? 2:03:19 PM
To:	Brenton Plourde (johnpauljones1979@)

Those will match my room perfectly! hahaha =]]

Sooo- I won't be responding to texts for a while. I unknowingly sat my phone in water today and my buttons don't work. I'm getting a new phone but, I have to chat that plan out with mother. I think I can still get phone calls but, I'm not sure. I did get you text today, though. So, howdy right back atcha.

yours,
Anna

From:	**Anna Guthrie** (anna_leigh_healer@)
Sent:	February 14, 200? 9:25:17 AM
To:	Brenton Plourde (johnpauljones1979@)

Hey-

In journo. my first newspaper came out today, I'm nervous as all get out. =]=] I'm sorry to hear about your favorite French singer. That sucks. Next year, I'm taking French One. So, I'll be able to kind of understand what you're saying when you speak it. You'll have to help me practice. I'll download those songs when I get home. Have a lovely day!

=]

Happy Valentines Day, btw.

Yours,
Anna

That is where it ends, on Valentine's Day 200?. The next night I get a text from Anna saying that she no longer wanted to talk and needs to take a step backwards in her life and be free for a while. I respect that. We have talked off and on since but to this day she holds a very special place in my heart. To cut and paste those was like cutting and pasting emotions that you previously had (and still have to a certain degree) and you are trying to get passed them and move on and you paste them back in (your heart and in your head) again. Does Anna actually exist? Possibly. Anna could be just a character

I made up for this book. Only Anna knows if she actually exists. It is now starting to become "window open longer season" and it feels good. I am a fan of stating the obvious or starting something that should or could lead into something constructive then just ending it—like that—what you just read. A lot of people these place a value on "material" things that they have and what their friends have: He has a car so he can come and pick me up or she works at Boston Astor's so she can get us free nachos but the true worth or value of someone is what they do not have—they don't have that will to never leave you when you are down, that will to love you even when you do not love yourself and to always be there when you need them. Every once in a while, people like Nataliya come along and while you may have different interests and tastes, I know that Nataliya will always be my Big Sister (even though I am a few years older than her) when I need her. They may be a flight away but they are always beside you.

It is not whether you win or lose; it is how good you look doing.

Shout out to my Little Sister Sam—keep up the good work! You have unbelievable worth and deserving—we are better for having you in our lives. We have all heard some great duets in our lifetime—Frank and Bono with "I've got You Under My Skin" to Elton John and Kiki Dee's "Don't Go Breaking My Heart" and the list goes on and on but for the first time here I have included a 'duet' section. This section is two poems that I and my Little Sister Sam have written together. These are called "Doits" and here is the first one:

> My sudden courage seemed to deflate
> I looked at her and she wanted to love me
> I can't think of anything
> I cannot think of anything to say to make this better
> My love for you, you want me to go find it?
> My heart, it saves messages
> You looked me, with a tear in your eye and shook your head

> I got up from the table
> And walked into the other room
> Put my hand on the door knob and hesitated—for a second.

I went to a website the other day and found that I only have another twenty-three years to live and well I am just fine with that. While people say that growing old is a good thing, I think I would like to accomplish everything in my life by the time I am 50 and then take the last 5 or so years off to relax. As of today, my almost 33 years of existence I have some grey hair but they are not that noticeable. I think I would like to age gracefully and be as important in life like say as Paul Newman—now there is a man who aged with grace and dignity, his hair did turn white but his eyes always stayed that magnificent blue. I should have applied my "50" Rule to that—what a bunch of bullshit? I should have just written the 50 pages and then took the last 5 pages or so and left them blank. So instead of looking for a job and improving my lifestyle as it appears this magazine I write for is going nowhere, I decided to make Brownies. It was hard work. They are in the oven now and well I am on break for the time being.

> Something tells me I want to be forever
> I want to be forever
> To be forever with you
> Something tells me I want to be with you
> Forever
> I want forever
> I want something forever with you
> Forever and a day.

> When spring blooms hope eternal
> When April showers bring flowers May -
> Be I will love you
> The leaves green with envy
> And the night time sky makes us stars

To the millions in the sky
Antiques walk hand in hand
Up and comers run freely
We sit and stare
And for a minute I wonder what my life
Would have been without you.

Hey! I won the right to Play Again at Tim Horton's! All right!

Why can't life come with a Guarantee or Warranty or Product Service Plan that say Future Shop has? I would gladly pay $49.99 for this Service Plan and when something in life is not working the way it should or is broken, I would take it back to Future Shop and get it exchanged for the exact same thing or it but a better model or something that will work—for me. I would send my heart away to get loving fixed at the depot but it will take two to three weeks. I got super lazy here and just cut and paste a previous paragraph from 50 pages ago, so enjoy the rerun. Devised plan. On Saturday afternoons I hang out in the local Walk—In Clinic in my town. I sit and flip through the magazines from last year, reading about who won the Super Bowl last year and how great I can look if I lose that extra 15 lbs. if I really applied myself at that time last year and be slimmer and more desirable at this time, one year from then. So I go there every Saturday afternoon and watch (secret agent man like) as the girls my age come in and take those pamphlets on certain diseases and how and what you can do to prevent it then I make mental notes to stay away from those ones when I see them at the club later on that night. The rerun is worse now than when I originally saw it. Shakespeare 200?:

Touch me not as I know no way of reciprocation
To stand naked but to be fully clothed in emotion
My lowered head
In shame and in defeat
Your eyes two swords
Of doubt

And devotion
Darkness, Darkness
For you cannot see
My heart shields
Any thoughts of civil war
I, the noble warrior
Ride off into your loving sunset
Horizon.

If only Monopoly money was real. In an effort to finish this book, I am going to start making obvious neutral observations—this is the Seinfeld book and it is about nothing. Every so often there will be a serious part in this book and here is a so often: Woke up yesterday with no feeling. Could not feel happiness or sadness. Felt weird—one dimensional. Being abused by my babysitter when I was younger has really started to affect me. I seem to not have the ability to make a connection between liking someone and actually LIKING someone. Speaking of someone, I worked up enough courage to send a message to Anna—perfect timing as well I could neither feel happy nor sad by the outcome. Surprisingly she did send one back but we have lost contact once again. I have a feeling this is going to be another long, hot summer.

Poetic champions compose
We write our own love story
We right our own love story
You bend my heart hardcover
I subscribe to your loving subscription
Twelve months is not enough
I have the day bookmarked
When I knew I loved you
You folded the top right corner
When you felt the same
Poetic champions compose
We write our own love story
We right our own love story

It is a shame that people cannot be friends due to circumstances within their control. There are many things I would like to accomplish in life and they are not the usual things like love, family, success etc. I have come up with a list:

[1] I would like to be an Ansel Adam's photograph.
[2] I would like to be a Paul Desmond solo.
[3] I would like to a Joao Miro painting.
[4] I would like to be an acted Marlon Brando part (though only from 1951 to 1958).

These are not lofty goals. Some nights, I dream that I am me. Most people dream that they are someone else but I dream I am me but just a worse version of real life me. Then when I wake up, I remember the dream and I feel better about myself.

Objects in your (bathroom) mirror are not smarter than they appear.

It is heading towards 11 AM on this Tuesday day in the beginning of June and I feel that I have accomplished nothing (though it is relatively early in the day). Every morning I wake up and start my day and then look at the clock at this time and feel the exact same way, which I guess repetitive feeling is accomplishing something. Bono and I agree: It's a beautiful day, don't let it get away, so I am off. Until we meet again. I sit abandoned in a hotel room. My phone still makes no sound. No internet, no Messenger, no Hotmail, no Facebook—no need. It appears none of my friends are "online" with where I am and how I feel and my emotion Inbox is empty.

The planes depart from the presidentially named airport
Destinations obscured by clouds
Business suite[s] for business (class)
Hotel sweets for extra-large heads
Cuff linked pressed shirts
Ties that loosen are the ties that bind

I am the airport man and I look out my own Observation Deck
My boreding pass says I leave in 20 minutes.

I have been living the Lazy First Dream today. I would like to tackle
some around the house jobs like CD reviews or continuing to write
this book. I have become Comfortably Numb. There is always an
interesting smell and I do use the term *interesting* loosely coming
from the downstairs apartment that exists in this house. It smells
like a combination of cooked potatoes and inexperience. According
to the trusted (again another loosely used term) Weather Channel,
today is going to be filled with a thunderous domestic dispute with
some tears. I am going start my open my own Weather Betting
Thing where I take bets on the weather. Things like if it will rain or
snow etc. and whomever is closest to the actual time that it starts to
rain or snow.

All I have ever been to someone is a wrong number.

The shower rains unsettled emotions upon me
The shower reigns with unsettled emotions upon me
I am not head and shoulders above the rest
I condition[er] myself for the worst
Replayed shower scene Psycho
You are not fully scream
Unless you are Zest fully scream
Singin' in the rain -
Every breath you take, every move you make
I'll be watching you.

Some rain coming down these last few days. I wonder of people have
stood outside during these rains and thought or felt like the piece I
included above. I do not think I could **redrum** anyone (hold mirror
up to page and read bolded word). Talked to anna_leigh_healer the
other day, she is good. She is getting ready to move to another town
for school. I know she will be a success—you can do it, put your
back into it. Just got back from doing nothing all day. It is very late

and I should be getting to bed but I have more nothing to do, there are not enough hours in the day to accomplish nothing. I may have to take a Saturday and do more nothing. Just checking my messages on my phone, no one called and they left a message—it was blank. It has been a long time since I have contributed anything to this and well it shows. I am finding the quality is going downhill. There should be a Quality Checker built into Microsoft Word like there is a Spell Checker that way when you write something, not only will it checks its spelling but also its quality as well. This will help all writers all around the world. No more unquality and more quality. Like for example, unquality is now read underlined squiggled and it is a word that does not exist but well to be honest it is a quality word so maybe this Quality Checker is no good. I should have invented it and used it about a paragraph and a half ago. Played in a land of robots and starships, stripped of my dignity, told to wash the moon with my toothbrush, I no longer felt invincible. I sang songs that made me happy, beep boop beep boop beep boop; All Request Hour is my savior.

I get a pencil because I feel it is a pencil that needs to be got
I tear out a piece of lined paper because I feel it is a piece of lined paper that needs to be torn out
I stare out my window for inspiration because I feel it is a window that needs to be stared out
I write words on the torn out piece of lined paper with the gotten pencil after I have looked out my window because I feel the need to write those words
I organize the words in a fashion that best suits the poem on the torn out piece of lined paper with the gotten pencil after I have looked out the window
You come into the room because you feel the room needs to be come into
You turn the television on because you feel the need to have the television on
You loudly open the bag of potato chips in the room that needed to be come into with the television that you felt needed to be on

You read over the poem that was written with the gotten pencil on the torn out lined piece of paper that was inspired by the open window with the words that were organized in such a fashion that best suits the poem in the room that you felt you needed to come into with the television you felt the need to have on with the loudly opened bag of chips and you place the poem beside you without a word of praise on the couch you felt needed to be sat on
I felt gotten, torn, stared at, fashion, come into, loudly, beside you I felt needed.

Feels like this shop should be closed for a while. Or, like in a movie when something major happens and then they "fast forward" to two year later—that is how this whole thing feels. So maybe this will be closed, locked up tight for a while and the "two years later" will appear.

Two Years Later.

When you go to College, you will meet a lot of people. These people will be in your classes or if you live in Residence these people will be your floor mates or people who live on other floors or other building and you are brought together by mutual love for alcohol, cards or Hockey Night in Canada. Most or say 99% of these friends will be "throw away friends" or "disposable friends" were you spend a "year" with them in College and then you guys go your separate ways and you never hear from them again. This is not the case for Natalija. Natalija has been a friend now for almost X years and it is nice to have that someone that you can rely on to give it you—straight good are in the bag. Here is the previously grandstanded big sister Natalija and this is what she is doing now:

Hello there

| From: | ☺**Natalija Perincic** (nattyperincic@) |
| Sent: | July 21, 200? 8:07:16 PM |

To:	johnpauljones1979@

Hey, how's it going?

Sorry I haven't been able to contact you sooner these past few weeks have been pretty hectic, and they will continue to be so until the end of August. Kenny and I have to find a new place to live, and I have a month to be out of my apartment so I've been searching for places, now I just have to make appointments to go view these cribs. LOL!

I miss you, I've been working a lot but also thinking about you a lot. How have you been? How is life back home. I'm not too sure when I will be coming home at this point, I also have to get a car because I've had a car since I was 16 and now I don't and it's killing me so I have to get on it, anything I can find quick you know just something to get me around the city because I'm so unhappy taking the bus and all I just dread it and I just can't seem to get over that feeling. I mean when I lived in Toronto it was a different story you know a BIG city with A LOT of people simply stressful to drive a car there plus Toronto's subway system is WAYY more advance than ours here in BLANKton. They are JUST NOW expanding the LRT which is what they call the subway system here, which I think is pretty gay, actually really gay like George Michael or Richard Simmons, however, I guess it makes sense since it's only goes underground 10% of the time. That was my rant on public transportation which I also think is GAY. Any new or exciting things you have to tell me about, if they are not new and exciting STILL TELL ME about them.

One of my best friends just recently moved to B.C. and I was sad we're close and she was one of my good friends. You know as you get older it's much harder to find good friends so you must keep all those ones you've had since you were in elementary school, however, the only problem with that is all of them are back home. I mean I have good friends here and I really enjoy their company but you know, it's not really the same, not the same AT ALL, so of course I miss everyone back home a lot.

We've had amazing weather here considering it IS summer, FACK. Except this past weekend was that huge rain storm we had, wow, was that ever crazy, did you get any of it back home, I heard that you did? However I may also be misinformed.

Well I want to hear or READ rather up on how you are doing. So email me back As soon as you can, it would be greatly appreciated.

I miss you and I love you and take care of yourself

Natty P.

Now personally, I like Public Transportation. Sure, sometimes it is a few minutes late but that just makes standing at the bus stop more fun—gives you a chance to read the posters that people hang in the little stations and judging by the way I am in a relationship, I may need a "Quick $300 Divorce." Natalija will always be there for me and I will always be there for her. It is great to have a sibling like Natalija in your life. For those who do not, get yourself some soon and for those who do, hold onto them like old baseball cards—put them in those plastic holders or plastic 9 card sheet binders and store them away forever.

Children live out their Olympic dreams
In backyard swimming pools
Barbeques simmer
With the sweet smell of success
A gentle breeze whispers gossip
From the neighborhood
Hushed tall tales of [in]decent affairs
And of plastic facial Barbie improvements
The stereo blasts the sounds of today
And the sounds of yesterday

I am here without you
Who dare steal my Sunshine?

Would like to have this next part telling you and showing you the wonderful e-mail that I got from **Anna** (anna_leigh_healer@) but alas there isn't one. That is okay, she will get around to it I am sure. Until then, I better come up with some great material for this slot. Bob Dylan was right—**the times are a changin'** and I do not know if I am ready for these changes quite yet. The world seems to be moving faster and faster these days and I am here, stuck in this time stoppage I call *myself*. Everything is new: new uPhone, new uPod, new tweeter and MyFace. I am Dylan acoustic while everyone else has gone Dylan electric. The only way this book is ever going to end is that I finish it. I highly doubt I will ever finish this at all. It has been two years, as you saw, since I really started writing anything. Now normally, in a two year span, things happen in people's lives and then they live to tell about them—I, on the other hand do not. Not because I do not like sharing the odd fable it is just nothing really exciting has happened. You would think someone who is writing something would have something to say? Maybe in another two years I will get married and have kids and settle down and have a nice house with a nice wife and a nice car and a nice job and a nice mortgage payment—I love the power of fiction.

The leaves changed out of their summer t-shirts and into their fall sweaters
Bright greens to reddish browns
The squirrels make a few extra trips to the chestnut Costco
Sometimes a mouthful isn't saying a lot
The dogs run around the park
Trying out their new fall coats
The birds cash in their Frequent Flyer Miles
For destinations known
No luggage lost
Free as a bird
I say to myself

Sixteen year old swingers swing
Sexual giggles on playgrounds
Since first built in 1979
Empty ball diamond
Holds 24 carat memories
Of games won and of games lost
You wear your hat just a little to the side
Your bag is big enough for Girlfriend in a Coma
You are beautiful
Since first built in 1985.

Aside from the Jazz Impression series a few pages back, none of these things really have titles. I wrote these on the bus below one day so these next ones all have the same title:

Mississauga Transit Bus #3E

If I drew a line in the sand and never crossed it, my feet would never get life dirty.

I don't feel like I will amount to anything and that's because everything in my life doesn't add up. I may never multiply and I always seem to subtract friends with what I say. I divide my time equally between love and hate. I am what I am. The equation is simple.

I just have paid the life fare. I sit in a seat that previously held thousands. I have the option to listen to my music, eat a sandwich or bring my dog with me. This transfer says I have until 3:15 PM to be someone else.

I am not the summer must see. I am not the big budget love story of the year. I am stored away in the closest and only shown on Thanksgiving. I am real too real. I am home movie.

I wish there was a sign on my heart that said to open push and hold bar on door. Shirt, no service.

Tea for one. One is the loneliest number. Just signed into the Hotmail.com machine and this is what I found amongst the many. Brought some real relief from the summer heat. Umbrella from the rain etc. Anna appears to have appeared back into my life. I do not how I feel about this:

From:	☺**Anna Guthrie** (anna_leigh_healer@)
Sent:	August 12, 200? 11:45:31 AM
To:	Brenton Plourde (johnpauljones1979@)
Traveled to the UP for the week, was in Canada briefly. =] Just thought I'd check up and say 'ello! All is well, hoping things are going the same your way. Extending love and hugs. Enjoy what's left of the summer! Are you published yet? yours, A	

If my heart had eyes it would see that you do not love me.

Sometimes things are best left untouched. Sometimes things are best left unsaid. Something things are best left not responded back to. Okay, the last one is a lie—I did respond back. Normalcy has kicked in. Thoughts and feelings have disappeared, well not disappeared but have been turned down from 8 to say 2 on The Like Meter. Good thing? Maybe, maybe not. Bad thing? Maybe, maybe not.

From:	☺**Anna Meyer** (anna_leigh_healer@)
Sent:	August 14, 200? 10:08:26 PM
To:	Brenton Plourde (johnpauljones1979@)

> Ohhhh, if only you could hear my Northern accent now, EH? hehehe Good to hear aboooot your book! I'm expecting a signed copy. =] Moving in about 2 weeks, excited yet scared to death. I've been off subweigh for a while now but, yes . . . I miss it tons!
>
> keep in touch, eh!
>
> A

Why do Americans think we say "aboooot" when we say "about" I mean if I meant a boot, I would say a aboot like I am going to kick their them in the ass with my about—I mean a boot, now I am confused. I keep freezing. I freeze in time. You know how you are watching a movie and say your DVD Player or Laptop "freezes?" Well that is what I am talking about. I freeze to over a year ago. The freezing I do actually coincides with the temperature of that time period. I want to skip forward to the next chapter of the movie but sometimes that is hard. I sometimes rewind and play out the scene again. I sometimes just push fast forward and watch how fast it all ends. Though to be honest, I cannot tell the difference between "fast forward" and "Play" and that is what pauses me. Thunderstorms go away, save your rain and your lighting displays for another day. Bring me relief in the form of a rain song. Hear me now, what did I say? The weather man never is right and well he never listens. People are starting to ask me if I want to get married or have children, which are only really brought on by the fact I will be thirty-three years old in a few months. Have not decided about any of these things as of yet—one girlfriend and one TLC 18 Kids and Counting Show at a time. Some fucking bullshit, some fucking bullshit, some fucking bullshit, some fucking bullshit, some fucking bullshit, some fucking bullshit. Heard sounds coming from the next room. If I do not come back, keep reading—I am sure you will get a kick out of what is ahead.

Thousands of hours and thousands of miles
Northern lights, Southern sites

Off the coast of the specific
Hand in hand
Heart in heart
David Gray on the radio
Coastal "Babylon"
God forbid that this never end
Flee from me, keeper of the Gloom
Suitcase makes a suite case
To stay
Unpacked emotions
Horizons of red
With a pinkish hue
Clouds form relationships
Love birds of a feather
Flock together
And hide their love away
Thousands of ours and thousands of smiles.

Like thieves in the night
We off stealing hearts
And breaking chandeliers
Along the way
Your love
Is a floppy boot stomp
In barn dances
Where the fiddler fiddles a tune
And I can look at you
And smile
Hands in my pockets
Glimpse into the future
Of attractions coming soon
This movie trailer
This move me, trail her
Don't let her get away
We stealing nights
Like thieves in the hearts.

I decided to go to the Library to finish this whatever it is. Might as well use up some of the power and resources that I pay for with my tax money. Since when can you not download porno at the main computer terminal?

Blah Blah Blah Blah Blah Blah Blah Blah Blah Blah Blah Blah Blah
Blah Blah Blah Blah Blah Blah Blah Blah Blah Blah Blah Blah Blah
Blah Blah Blah Blah Blah Blah Blah Blah Blah Blah Blah Blah Blah
Blah Blah Blah Blah Blah Blah Blah Blah Blah Blah Blah Blah Blah
Blah Blah Blah Blah Blah Blah Blah Blah Blah Blah Blah Blah Blah
Blah Blah Blah Blah Blah Blah Blah Blah Blah Blah Blah Blah Blah
Blah Blah Blah Blah Blah Blah Blah Blah Blah Blah Blah Blah Blah
Blah Blah Blah Blah Blah Blah Blah Blah Blah Blah Blah Blah Blah
Blah Blah Blah Blah Blah Blah Blah Blah Blah Blah Blah Blah Blah
Blah Blah Blah Blah Blah Blah Blah Blah Blah Blah Blah Blah Blah
Blah Blah Blah Blah Blah Blah Blah Blah Blah Blah Blah Blah Blah
Blah Blah Blah Blah Blah Blah Blah Blah Blah Blah Blah Blah Blah
Blah Blah Blah Blah Blah Blah Blah Blah Blah Blah Blah Blah Blah
Blah Blah Blah Blah Blah Blah Blah Blah Blah Blah Blah Blah Blah
Blah Blah Blah Blah Blah Blah Blah Blah Blah Blah Blah Blah Blah
Blah Blah Blah Blah Blah Blah Blah Blah Blah Blah Blah Blah Blah
Blah Blah Blah Blah Blah Blah Blah Blah Blah Blah Blah Blah Blah
Blah Blah Blah Blah Blah Blah Blah Blah Blah Blah Blah Blah Blah
Blah Blah Blah Blah Blah Blah Blah Blah Blah Blah Blah Blah Blah
Blah Blah Blah Blah Blah Blah Blah Blah Blah Blah Blah Blah Blah
Blah Blah Blah Blah Blah Blah Blah Blah Blah Blah Blah Blah Blah
Blah Blah Blah Blah Blah Blah Blah Blah Blah Blah Blah Blah Blah
Blah Blah Blah Blah Blah Blah Blah Blah Blah Blah Blah Blah Blah
Blah Blah Blah Blah Blah Blah Blah Blah Blah Blah Blah Blah Blah
Blah Blah Blah Blah Blah Blah Blah Blah Blah Blah Blah Blah Blah
Blah Blah Blah Blah Blah Blah Blah Blah Blah Blah Blah Blah Blah
Blah Blah Blah Blah Blah Blah Blah Blah Blah Blah Blah Blah Blah
Blah Blah Blah Blah Blah Blah Blah Blah Blah Blah Blah Blah Blah
Blah Blah Blah Blah Blah Blah Blah Blah Blah Blah Blah Blah Blah
Blah Blah Blah Blah Blah Blah Blah Blah Blah Blah Blah Blah Blah
Blah Blah Blah Blah Blah Blah Blah Blah Blah Blah Blah Blah Blah

Blah Blah Blah Blah Blah Blah Blah Blah Blah Blah Blah Blah Blah
Blah Blah Blah Blah Blah Blah Blah Blah Blah Blah Blah Blah Blah
Blah Blah Blah Blah Blah Blah Blah Blah Blah Blah Blah Blah Blah
Blah Blah Blah Blah Blah Blah Blah Blah Blah Blah Blah Blah Blah
Blah Blah Blah Blah Blah Blah Blah Blah Blah Blah Blah Blah Blah
Blah Blah Blah Blah Blah Blah Blah Blah Blah Blah Blah Blah Blah
Blah Blah Blah Blah Blah Blah Blah Blah Blah Blah Blah Blah Blah
Blah Blah Blah Blah Blah Blah Blah Blah Blah Blah Blah Blah Blah
Blah Blah Blah Blah Blah Blah Blah Blah Blah Blah Blah Blah Blah
Blah Blah Blah Blah Blah Blah Blah Blah Blah Blah Blah Blah Blah
Blah Blah Blah Blah Blah Blah Blah Blah Blah Blah Blah Blah Blah
Blah Blah Blah Blah Blah Blah Blah Blah Blah Blah Blah Blah Blah
Blah Blah Blah Blah Blah Blah Blah Blah Blah Blah Blah Blah Blah
Blah Blah Blah Blah Blah Blah Blah Blah Blah Blah Blah Blah Blah
Blah Blah Blah Blah Blah Blah Blah Blah Blah Blah Blah Blah Blah
Blah Blah Blah Blah Blah Blah Blah Blah Blah Blah Blah Blah Blah
Blah Blah Blah Blah Blah Blah Blah Blah Blah Blah Blah Blah Blah
Blah Blah Blah Blah Blah Blah Blah Blah Blah Blah Blah Blah Blah
Blah Blah Blah Blah Blah Blah Blah Blah Blah Blah Blah Blah Blah
Blah Blah Blah Blah Blah Blah Blah Blah Blah Blah Blah Blah Blah
Blah Blah Blah Blah Blah Blah Blah Blah Blah Blah Blah Blah Blah
Blah Blah Blah Blah Blah Blah Blah Blah Blah Blah Blah Blah Blah

That is a transcript of a recent conversation I had with my parents.
As you can see, it pertains to them wanting me to be successful and
make something of my life—not sit around all day watching Night
Court and writing a book. How successful do they want me to be?
What should I do with my life? Writing a book for say another
hour a day was being successful and making something of myself?
It is not the Hemingway, it is not the Himmingway, and it is the
Myingway.

Something tells me the lion sleeps tonight
And the lamb lies down on Broadway
Type cast as a poor man's banker
I save no penny
Would you marry me anyway?

Habitat for humanity
House of cards
Filled with a Joker
And a Queen - of
Diamonds - she had
And boy they sparkled
In the morning light.

Viewer discretion is advised. Have you been modified from your original version and have been formatted to fit the "life" screen. If people were watching your life, like say the same premise as a season of oh Real World: You or Big Brother, what disclaimer would they put up on the screen? The classic: Warning, the following program contains scenes of nudity, sexuality and coarse language, view discretion is advised or this film is rated G for General Audiences—Do you think you could be or are that innocent? Are you a well-drawn Disney classic?

I wrote this to tell you how I feel
Then I folded it into a paper airplane
Origami time machine
Looking back on the future
I threw it out the window
Emotion boomerang
With hopes it was scheduled land
In your hand runway
As you looked up at my window
Some sunny day baby
Everything seems okay baby
My love jet
Is scheduled to take off
Clearance from your heart tower
Is all I need.

I guess you can kinda tell who this book is dedicated to. She, along with my "sister" Natalija, has had the biggest impact on my life.

I wish I could be around all of them every day. Get your Kleenex box and get yer ya ya's out! We got some sadness followed by some happiness to come. I cannot guarantee that but I will try. I should put that at the end of every "relationship" conversation I have with women from this day forward.

Don't talk to me like lovers do, be with me like lovers be.

Had a life changing experience yesterday and since well it is always suggested that you talk about your feelings and things that bother you, this page will be dedicated to that except well no mention of actually what happened will well be mentioned. This change was brought upon an experience that would leave someone in total fear. It lasted for about 3 hours and it is something that people should never experience. When taking a long time to become more of an extrovert, this experience soon slams the door shut and the introvert elephant looms large in the room. Says here that a certain President has a gay lover—so what? Don't we all? We all (apparently) have a twin who lives somewhere else in the world, so I am sure we all can have a gay lover now and then. Every day is a struggle to find a useful place for oneself. Feeling like the token not fit in the fit in worklifeplace is something that people should discover once and the try not to discover if again. Never dream about dreaming. They never come through—none of them.

Stop the rain from falling
Large puddles
Are a dance floor revolution
Umbrella Rihanna
You give me shelter
Pail shelter
Bale out this boat load of emotions
Titanic
Hug me like a life jacket
Sail me down
The sea of love.

A lot of my life is being alone. You know when you are on Facebook and there is no one on to talk to—that is me and no one is available to chat. When I was a kid, I did not have a wild imagination, I just thought of things that were imaginarily wild:

For the longest time I thought my Dad was Freddie Mercury. Every morning (granted I was 5 years old and this was 1981) my Dad would get up and comb his Freddie Mercury moustache and get ready for work. Then I would see my Dad on television, parading around in the latest Queen video. I found out later that my Dad was not Freddie Mercury—all I have to say is Another One Bites The Dust.

I created a Group on Facebook called "The Most Popular and Well Known Guy in the World" and well I am the only member. I update it every week with pictures of myself sitting at the same computer desk, just wearing different clothes. I am the Administrator and even though my Group is available to the public, I have my life set on private.

I have my window. Every now and then I open the curtains to see what is outside. It is as if someone has painted each season, using oil and acrylic paints, and has hung the picture in front of my window. The Bob Ross style tree looks lonely out there. Someone should paint him a friend. I would be jealous.

The inability to communicate with others is something I appear to lack. Sometimes I like to talk a walk in the neighborhood. Passing people, walking with their dogs on a leash or with their children on small bicycles, they nod at me to say "Hello" or give the smile but I just tend to look at the ground. I count the spokes on the bike tires or I count the legs on the dog.

The kids are running around, screaming in the park close to my house. The adults are running around, screaming in the houses close to the park. Relationships are new to me. There is a certain fear I harbor that I would never make a great boyfriend or a great husband. My non job at IBM is causing to be a workaholic and I have no time for my so make believe wife and my make believe kids. The real dog needs to go outside.

Thirty is the new thirty. People now feel that if you have not accomplished any of your goals by the time you are thirty then you might as well pack it in and work at the local CD/DVD/GAMER Megastore close to your house. Women used to judge men by their shoes but no a days they judge them by their tie.

My hair is starting to turn white. Not grey but white. I could run a brush through it but what is the use? It will all probably fall out. Stress is one factor for losing one's hair. I am not stressed so much about life or work or love or rent, I am stressed that someone will see me on the street and mistake me for Steve Martin. I am the lonely guy.

Tried internet dating once and it did not go as planned. It is like you meet the opposite sex equivalent of yourself. That cleverly matched person is just like you: same favorite television shows, same favorite music artists, same favorite movies and same favorite places to meet people on the internet because like you, they do not have anyone. For the $50 a month this website is charging me, I could go to a Singles Dance at my local Legion and sit and download mentally all the other unattached and unloved people within 100 kilometers from me. I could never upload a picture introduction of myself to these single people as well but my life and heart only runs on 56 kbps. That will take too long and in today's world people seem to download who they want and then delete them from their heart memory hard drive faster than you can say IPOD.

Everyday someone deletes me from their Friend section on Facebook. I do not mind this as well I may not leave any sort of message or really contribute anything to their lives other than being a number on the right hand side of their Facebook page. Here now is a list of Friends numbers I have been: 247, 26, 89, 104 and 17. Maybe someday I will be a number one on someone's list.

Sometimes I dream at night that I am lying beside someone who cares for me. My bed is a double bed and right now I have free reign over the whole entire thing. People tend to shift in their beds and take all the sheets and blankets from the other person in order to feel warm and secure. I always make sure I leave some extra sheet and blanket on the other side of the bed in case one night my dream comes true.

Maybe I could be a Big Brother. Take some time out of my busy life and adopt a 'tween' boy and do things that I may not have done when I was younger like baseball games and other things that boys and their big brothers do. I remember once when I played baseball when I was younger in an organized city baseball league and it was two outs bottom of the ninth and we needed one run to win. Our coach looked down the bench and saw me sitting at the end, my glove beside me, my hat sitting just right on my head. This is a situation every boy dreams about: two outs, bottom of the ninth, runner on third and all we needed was a base hit to win the game. Put me in coach, I'm ready to play. He called Margaret's name.

The burning desire is there. Though the fire is small and continues to get smaller, the burning desire is still there. I would like to be more open, more out there, participating in conversations at local hot spots about art and poetry, music, movies and the art of poetry and the art of music and the art of movies and acting. The scenes take place in my head. I should be the star but I am just an extra, standing alone in the background. Inconspicuous.

Recently came across some of those "Worst Dating Disaster Clips" on YouTube. Now, I have this major fear that I would be one of those people in the compilation clips if I were to try a Dating Service like that. Finding the right thing to say to try and impress someone would not be my strong point. It is like selling something you do not believe in. Confidence plays a major role in this dating/selling of yourself and I am afraid that I do not possess this plus I do not photograph well anyways, so I have a feeling even though I am 175 lbs., I would come off as a John Goodman body double.

Set the table tonight for dinner. Normally I would only set the table for one person but tonight I set it for two. Two plates, two sets of forks and knives and spoons, two glasses of Pepsi and two napkins. I even put some pasta with sauce on the second plate and made an extra few pieces of garlic bread in case someone came to the door and I could invite them in for dinner. While the bell in my head went off as this could be a good idea, the door bell has not.

I want to go to my own funeral. Okay, I know that is impossible but I have an idea: I would find a person with the same name as me and attend their funeral. The reason in doing this would be to see firsthand how my own funeral may be. Would these people be my friends if that was me? Getting all technical, the answer would be no but I would like to think you may get an idea of who your friends are/would become based on the attendance though I have a feeling that no one would show up. Just because my name and his name are the same would that mean him and me, no matter what age would have had the same friends. Would one friend be a banker? Would one friend be an unemployed landscaper with a family to feed; a dog to feed and a loan shark to feed? It is about the quality of the people who are there. Being there would be like looking in a mirror that gives you a reflection of yourself but also is a portal for a dimension that relates to you but the characters are different—but they could be the same.

Heard a sad song on the radio today. Kind of felt like I had written it; played all the instruments and sang it the same way it was played on the radio. This song lasted about four minutes long. I have a feeling mine would just be about three seconds. You know that sound at the beginning of a store bought cassette/album that signifies that the music is about to start—that would be my sad song. I wish I could signify when something good is about to happen. Though in all reality, you know when the tape is done and the music fades out and the tape just stops and all you hear is silence? That would be me. It would final. Do not bother to flip it over. It is blank.

Being the same height since you were in your early teens is a way to measure your growth. I am not talking about actual height but I am. When you look at pictures of yourself through the years you can see your different heights and how much your stock in life has grown—gained value. It is like those stock market shows you see on television where they show you an up and coming stock, how the line is growing, moving upwards on a somewhat steady path, with highs and plateaus from the left to the right. Think of yourself as that stock as you look upon the older pictures of yourself. You have gained (life and love) value and while you may have reached your set life height you do continue to grow in value and soon, yes, your growth will turn to decline and then someday your stock in life may not be as valuable as it once was. Since I have been the same height since my early teens it feels as though I have not gained any value or have not increased in any value at all. You can see the constant straight line over the years if you were to look at the photos. While I am alive, it appears as though I have flat lined 20 years ago. You should have sold me then.

Every morning I watch the sunrise and every night I watch the sun go down. Sometimes I wonder if I have a twin on the other side of the world and if he is looking out his window, doing what I am doing except it would be the opposite. Would this twin have the same thoughts as me? Would he feel happy when I feel sad and would he feel sad when I feel happy? If I parted my hair on the left, would he part his on the right? I feel alone. He must feel that too.

Looking out my window I see leaves running across the lawn. Like friends, on a pub crawl on a Saturday night, they are in a hurried fashion—only stopping when the winds of change have died down. Sometimes life is like that, you grow up from the tree, you leave the tree and you go out on the lawn of the world. You get raked up in life, love and happiness/unhappiness and when you get burnt, the smell of success is not all that sweet.

Back in 1971, The Band (Robbie Robertson, Richard Manual, Garth Hudson, Rick Danko and Levon Helm) released a song called *Life is a Carnival.* Life is a carnival it seems, we go on different roller coasters of emotions—sometimes you are up and sometimes you are down and those emotions are the price you pay. Everything is not cotton candy nor is it winning teddy bears. For the longest time I thought it was Life is a Carnivore, where you are the meat and life chews you up, swallows you and spits you out again. I have been heartbroken, so I have been hit with the tenderizing hammer and have added a bit of desperation sauce. Turn me over, I am done.

Phone rang this afternoon. It was a telemarketer selling me something I did not need like a steak knife set or more digital cable channels or something like that. She was very nice, she told me who cutting edge it all was—so it was either were knives or digital cable channels—and how much it would benefit me in life. She said that if I had company over and I was entertaining on a Saturday evening, whatever she was selling would come in handy. I could save a lot of time and money by order whatever it was she was selling from her. It would be an upgrade from what I originally have/had and that people would be in awe of me and want whatever it was for their own. I found myself looking at my credit card. For a minute there she almost had me. She had a convincing voice. It was just nice to talk to someone.

For the longest time I thought my Dad was Howard Hesseman. Every morning (granted I was 6 years old and this was 1982) my Dad would get up and comb his Howard Hesseman moustache and get ready for work. Then I would see my Dad on television, working at WKRP in Cincinnati and talking on the radio. I found out later that my Dad was not Dr. Johnny Fever—all I have to say is Alright fellow babies!

Talking or writing about what bothers you apparently is supposed to make you feel better. Well in fact, I feel worse. I read over what I wrote say two pages ago and it reminds how I was say two days ago and now I feel much worse than I did say two minutes ago.

Every day I check my Friends List on Facebook to see if it decreases by one or two overnight, when I am asleep and am not aware of this deletion of friendship and do not have a chance to argue my case of why I am your friend and to make my friendship with you better. To see the number decrease each day or every other day is not really heart breaking at all. Sometimes it is a good thing. It means I have less things to remember (like your birthday or to congratulate you on your new job or new boyfriend) and even the keeping up of a conversation on our Walls. I always delete my Wall every month because those conversations are old, they have had their time, been talked about, analyzed and confirmed and denied and have been sealed away in a non-confidential envelope for the rest of our lives.

Hate seems to be a strong word. I hate myself. Coming to this hating conclusion is probably the only thing I like about myself. I made a decision. Every day I just sit here and do nothing. I contribute nothing to society and I have no friends. Let me rephrase that, I have very few friends but they are off being friends with my other friends and I am not. It generally is two or three days that I go without talking to someone. I will leave a message, write a letter, send an e-mail and no one responds. I keep the Kleenex Company afloat. I also keep TVO afloat as well.

Not that someone asked me this question but this question I asked myself as I was about to fall asleep and that was: How would I like to die? And the simple answer is I would like to just close my eyes and never wake up. I would not have to be old, I could be the age I am now and just go to bed knowing that when I close my eyes, I am never waking up again.

Now this has lead me to this question: What would be the last thing I would like to see before I close my eyes? I do not know as of right now. I would imagine it would be watching one of my favorite television shows or a concert DVD from one of my favorite bands and just reading a letter from a close friend telling me how good they are doing and how their boyfriend has finally smartened up and is treating her better and how excited she is to be done her first year of University—you know that kind of thing.

Something else that I have thought about before I close my eyes is that now I go to sleep thinking that my biological father will call me the next day. Of course, this never happens and well I am not mad or glad or sad because I know he never will. I find now that I am getting older I would like to "show" my biological father what I have accomplished in life. I am aware that this mode of thinking is different from the normal mode where when you are younger you want to know who your parent or parents are and then the older you get, you just subside or live up the "fuck it" or "fuck him/her/them" attitude but for me, I am reversed. While I may have accomplished some things in life that, to me, are noteworthy and may be worth sharing with my biological father, I think I will always just hold onto that falling asleep each night with one ear open, waiting for the phone to ring.

I tend to erase things, not only from Facebook and/or e-mail but from my head drive as well. Someone was asked me to remember a phone number and while I am very good at remembering numbers, the phone number and the person attached or assigned or inherited with that phone number meant nothing to me, so I forgot it. I did remember it at one time but since that person has up and sold the farm and left me as a friend, I forgot it. People always ask me or say to me "Remember the time when we laughed at . . ." well I do not remember those times at all. I chose to delete them actually. Those "Summer Laughs 2009" files do not mean anything to me anymore. I deleted the pictures and the text file that held the dialogue. The past laugh is now a present tear.

Noticed recently that the veins on the tops of my hands have become more and more prevalent. Maybe these veins are now the constructed roads in which my thoughts now have a direct route or highway to my fingers which in turn type these thoughts out onto my lap top. My hands appear to be getting smaller as well, maybe I am just shrinking in my not even old age as of yet. My hands are getting smaller because I am sick. Too bad these hands could not clap at my own funeral. Job well done the clapping would signify.

*I traced the line on my left with my right index finger and well the path lead me nowhere.

I stand at my window, in my bedroom, on the second floor and look down the street from right to left. I sometimes see people walking on the sidewalks either on my side of the street or on the other side. I want them to look up at me and wave, just so it feels like I have friends. They do not really have to be my friends; they can just walk by everyday day or two or every week and wave to me. I know I would smile and I would wave back. Sometimes it is good to have friends who are always on the move—keeps you grounded and I already am.

I died today. Thank-you for not coming to my funeral. The service was short and the sandwiches were even shorter. The eulogy was read by the woman who embalmed me. It was only three sentences and two of them she made up off the top of her head.

Street sounds
Are like garbage cans orchestras
They are conducted by conductors
Most likely conducting inappropriate conduct
The lids
They rattle and hum
Sweet sounds
To those whose musical tastes
Are deep rooted in the steel drums behind restaurant buildings

Boulevard musicianship
Is where the cool "cats" hangout
And the "Rat" Pack scurry about
From one gig to the next
Suite sounds
We listen from our balcony windows
Most nights, it is incidental music
Far off distant sounds
One block (chords) to the next block (chords)
I have some sympathy
For their symphony
And the Trash Can Sinatra's
Sing me to sleep at night.

It was a night of lonesome January
Twenty-three days
The sound of silence
Was even too loud for the deaf
Window, window
Mirrors his rejection
Reflection
Of a man once content
Contents
Of a book filled with words to express
How he felt for her
For love,
He asked no quarter
She threw pennies from heaven
He was rich in her love.

August
Oh, how the leaves did -
Fall, 2007
You held my hand
It felt like
Winter, 2006

It was cold
You were mad and I was glad
I had
No idea
We shared the same bed once
You slept close to me
In the middle
Uncomfortable because I slept on the -
Spring, 2006
Warmth and the late evening
We sat on the curbs
Just left of the street lamps
And counted the stars
Summer here, summer there
Emotions -
Some are now.

Her glasses allow her
To see right through me
Bifocals, by focus
The black frames
Hold us together
Her love is set to no prescription
She lens her heart to me
I want it forever

The Merry-Go-Round
Merrily went 'round
The wind swept leaves
Were like little red and brown hands
Waving good-bye
As they went off into the sunset
The price of [her] admission
Made was quiet
I was Marcel Marceau

She sings to me
Like Sarah Vaughan used to
Live on stage
At Carnegie Hall
'Round Midnight
Embraceable Me
Embraceable she
Ashleigh, to me
Is like April in Paris
It Might As Well Be Spring
She is my
September Song
Autumn Leaves
A Lover's Concerto
Is what she sounds like
When she says she loves me
She moved through the Autumn Fair
Her hands in her pockets
Her tears like summer streams
Her heart on sleeve
The price of her admission
She stopped to look up only once
When she heard me say
"I love you."

I sometimes sit and wonder what it would be like to be a published author—no matter how "big" or "small" you get. Okay, so your book is published—great. Would you walk into your local "big box book store" and go to the Fiction section and see that there are 3 copies of your book on the shelf on say a Thursday afternoon and then by Tuesday of the following week, would you go back and see if there are three copies still sitting on that shelf? What if there were only two? Did someone buy your book? Did that person stand there for a few minutes on a Saturday, in the early evening, and flip through your book and think that this may be a good read and then purchased your book? HOW EXCITING! YOU ARE A SUCCESS!

A PURCHASE! A ROYALITY CHEQUE! .76 CENTS! But then thoughts of what if someone picked it up, sat somewhere within the store, read say three pages, thought it was total garbage, got up and left the book on the chair—right where not only their ass was but countless other asses as well were—like your book is full of shit, just like all those other asses.

New moon fortune teller says
We will all be stars
We have
Kennedy suspicions
Nickel, penny jars
Mix tapes and sound scapes
Heart rates
And a quiet wall of sound
We live in muddy waters
But we ain't got the blues
We are -
The joy division
We sit red faced at stop signs
And wander outside the white lines
The grass, is green with envy
Hear our battle cries
We sink yellow submarines
We tell
Neither truth nor lies
Running scared
We are the Picassos of the night
We brush off exhilaration
We got
Neither tears nor fears
Christians to the lions
Holy water
Rains down on the churches
Rains down on the parishioners
Rains down on the Popes

Look into our eyes
Feel it in our sly
We got
High Hopes.

It can be seen far and wide
How narrow the mind
To count the grains
The sands of time
Tick, Tock, Tick, Tock
Into the distance
Hold your hand up
To shield you
From the sun
Squinted eyes
Can see far and wide
How narrow the mind
To count the grains
The sands of time
Tick, Tock, Tick Tock
No explanation
All imagination
On the cover of Time Magazine
Turn the page
Magnified
It can be seen far and wide
How narrow the mind
Copyrighted
Name domains
To count the grains
The sands of time
The unexplained -
We shall
Take it back someday
Tick, Tock, Tick, Tock.

The silence is listening
To our boasts of futures
And of our pasts
We are
Earmarked for success
Put on your jacket
Put on your hat
We out the door
Before they awake
Sit, quietly
The silence is listening
We whisper loudly
Tell'em like it is
We make up stories
History, as we go
We are natural born killers
I shot the sheriff
And you will shoot the deputy
Grab my hand, Thelma
Louise needs you tonight
We drive off the 102.1
The Edge
Alternative to what we know
And to what they have seen
You whisper in my ear that you love me
The listening is silent.

There is a five inch gap between my curtains
In my window
I cannot see left
And I cannot see right
My view is straight forward
Through the trees
Past the roof tops
Over the hills
And far away

A black power line
Sometimes acts like a horizon
Though while the sun does not set there
I feel closer to the end of the world
A bird arrives in a tree
And soon will branch out to a different destination
He just stopped to pick up some things
At the Pine Needle Convenience Store
I am stranded on a desert island
Snowed in
Alone
And my window of opportunity
Has no apply happiness pie
On the sill
This play has ended
The curtain closes
I now can see what is left
And what is right.

Like blankets
Dark themes
Cover the beds of subconscious
We take no comfort[er]
In the sheets [of deception]
We hold up to our faces [lessness]
Late at night
[Late at day]
The written word poets
Speak frail Braille
To those who listen
With [out] intent
'Round of applause
Around of apt laws
Forcibly confine
Those who are all free [dom]
We right about what we know

We right about what we see
We right about what we hear
And we right about what we feel
We are
Writers on the Storm.

And now an interview conducted by this author to this author. This interviewed is author-ized.

Interviewer: "Hello, thank-you for taking time out of your busy day to do this interview."

Interviewee: *"It was no trouble. I am glad that someone wanted to interview me."*

Interviewer: "Okay, let's start. Where were you born?"

Interviewee: *"In a medium sized town, two hours north of Toronto, Ontario."*

Interviewer: "That is in Canada, correct?"

Interviewee: *"Yes, that is correct."*

Interviewer: "What made you want to become a writer?"

Interviewee: *"I guess just had all these thoughts and ideas rolling around in my head, so I decided to put them down on paper one day."*

Interviewer: "Was your family supportive of you becoming an author and not say a mechanic or a tradesman of some sort?"

Interviewee: *"They were. One of the best things about coming from the medium sized town or city I am from is the wanting to get out of it—and while I may have lived there for the first 16 years of my life, I had already left it mentally and visually long before that. So my family understood the value of wanting to break free from any confines, whether they are physically, economically or mentally and the want of making some more of yourself."*

Interviewer: "Says here you went to college and attained a diploma in journalism. Did that help in anyway?"

Interviewee: *"It teaches you structure and the ability to self-edit. You learn how to cut back on certain aspects within the context of a story—a news story—that while may be important, the information may not be as important as you thought."*

Interviewer: "You worked for a time in radio. How was that different from putting pen to paper?"

Interviewee: *"You are vocal. You learn to express yourself through the vocal form. You learn how to time everything—whether it is song play or how to use 12 seconds to its full advantage."*

Interviewer: "You also wrote about jazz music. You were one of those jazz critics?"

Interviewee: *"No. Out of all the CDs I have ever reviewed, I think I only ever wrote three negative reviews. I do not play an instrument so who am I to judge the artist's piano playing? I mean they are out there, they are doing it, they are making albums and playing gigs. They are living their dreams, so who am I to say that their playing is not up to par when I do not even play piano myself."*

Interviewer: "Are you currently writing anything?"

Interviewee: *"Yes, this interview."*

Like an old chessboard at a garage sale
I have a checkered past
With "L" shaped movements—the "L" standing for life
I was rooked into believing I would be something—someone
Then I was crowned King—Nothing
I'm on the outside looking in
The mirror of inception
Reflects a transparency
That I cannot see myself
Kicking down
The doors of reception
Unhinged
I open the window

And crawl through to the closet
This then dens my feelings
And puts myself and my feelings in basement
Right next to the attic—lofty
I was one Knight away -
From calling it a day.

I have a feeling I am just going to have pages and pages of poems.
I do not know if a book has been a mish mash of poems then text
then poems then text. Maybe I am not a good writer at all. I mean I
kind of feel like say Mall Security. I was not good enough to become
a Police Officer so I become Mall Security instead I guess I am [s]
Mall [in]Security.

I see people raking leaves.
It is like they are collecting all these thoughts, emotions and hurts
into one big pile and then bagging them up and getting rid of
them—to the curb.
I hear the sirens.
It is like the Policemen and women are yelling at the top of their
lungs "Get out of the way! Robbery! Shots fired! Shots fired!" as the
rush down the streets and rush down the highways.
The water drains down the sink.
It is like all the little water droplets are Japanese people, getting on
the subway during the rush hour each day, filling up the subway
platforms and being crammed in the subway cars—down the tube
and off they go.

Everything is in motion.
Everyone and/or has a place to go and/or people to see. When I
look out my window it is like a television screen and I am watching
a movie and it is on fast forward. They want to make it to their
destinations - the credits screen.
The furnace kicks in.
But I don't.

Paint the sun
Paint the moon
Wallpaper the sky
Add the trees
Like Bob Ross used to
Shadow puppet the birds
Origami the boats
Pencil ruler the horizon
Kraft Dinner Noodle me
Put me as ease—l.

How lonesome is the bird
Who flies by night?
Who fearsome is the tiger
Who hunts by night?
How handsome is the man
Who lies by night?
How troublesome is the girl
Who cries by night.

First impression
Second thoughts
Third string quarter back
Fore scorn (and seven years ago)
Take Five
New at Six
Seven steps to heaven
Eight (minutes without you) is enough.

It was the best of times
It was the worst of times
It was -
Once upon a time
When you loved me
Victory
So sign of defeat

Then you left me
Trampled under foot
Those boots were made for walking
(De feet).

My heart
Flows continuously with unhappiness
Damon's A River Runs Through It
It Afflecks me
Makes me sad
I cast my loving line
Into the stream
Plenty of Fish
I wait
A tug, a pull
In hopes of love
A Moby Dick of love
All I reel in
Is the rubber boot.

Empty
Full of
Empty
Cast off
Alone
Cast of
Thousands
Memories
Memories
Of forgetting
Amnesia
Who I am?
I remember now
I am . . .

. . . Man, I have written a lot of poems. Are they any good? Who judges poems? Who is the one that says "That is great!" or "That is shit!" and why can I not have that job? I would always base the grade on the "Roses are red, violets are blue . . ." and if your poem did not move me in the manner of "Roses and red, violets are blue . . ." then you have some work to do.

There have been books
And there have been books
Magazines, Mega Zines
Telling truth less slander
Fiction, f[r]iction
Spreading lies like a
Proper Gandhi
Propaganda
Autobiographies
Automatic for the people
The power is the spoken word
In the written word
Hardcover your heart
Everybody hurts
Sometimes
So hold on.

The winds of change
Oh! How they Howl
Like weather parentals
The yell down the corridors
And through the trees
For once I seek solace in the sun
I need the Allen key to release me
But the winds of change
Still Howl at me
Ginsberg me
Stab me
In the back

Not my street
Not my town
8:13 P.M.
Darkness
Hands in pockets
Face in sheepishly
An owl asked me
Who?
I said pardon.
Who?
I said a girl.
Who?
I said it did not matter her name.
Who?
Okay, her name is Victoria.
Who?
She and I were seeing each other.
Who?
Me.
Who?
Who am me, I asked?
Who?
I do not know, I said.
Why? Said the owl
And with that I walked off
I turned back to look at the owl
But he was gone.

For the longest time I thought my Dad was Ken Wregget—goalie for the Toronto Maple Leafs. Every morning (granted I was 12 years old and this was 1988) my Dad would get up and comb his Ken Wregget moustache and get ready for work. Then I would see my Dad on television, stopping pucks on Hockey Night in Canada. I found out later that my Dad was not Ken Wregget—and the Leafs would never win the Stanley Cup without him.

Beautiful smile
Three vowels
In her name
And she is
All "A's"
To me
She has blonde
Ambition
Madonna
Her thoughts
And love
Vogue
They dance upon
The dance floors
Of sparkled happiness
And of wood paneled emotion
Her beautiful smile
Lights up my life
Like a thousand disco balls.

COATA

This morning I took the 'A' train. Okay, it wasn't the 'A' train, it was the #3 Bus but to me, it had the same rhythm. Even though the bus went from point A to be B and turned around and then went from point B to point A and did that until it is prescribed time off and then started up again the next morning, I wanted to go further. I had a Transfer. The bus driver gave me one when I paid my $3.00 "sir" charge. Every so often I would look out the window for change—even though I took this bus every day, in both directions, I would look for change but the song remains the same.

Every once in a while, I would see a small glimpse of change—someone walking down the street, another house up for sale, a garbage can which appeared to be abandoned for days but for the most part everything stayed the same. It is like buying a CD and playing it once and hearing it and then not hearing it for a week and then playing it again, sure, you may hear something different—a bass line or drum part you did not hear before, but it was always there—the CD did not change musical content from say rock to classical overnight or when you were not looking, stalled in the bathroom.

Conclusions and assumptions are the easiest thing to do in life. This is an easy conclusion and assumption I just made/came up with—see how easy they are. Often conclusions and assumptions are based on our own way of how it should be, not always supported by rock solid facts or pie charts or statistic books—just our own self-centered conspiracy theories.

The suspension on this bus is faulty. I feel like I am being thrown around like one of those kids in the those air filled castles that parents rent for their child's birthday and I am standing on one end and someone jumps up and down on the other—the shock waves are minor but it is enough for an earthquake headache later. There is an abandoned arm chair on the side of the road, out for garbage. Sometimes when I see them I just want to sit in it with my potato chips, a can of pop and a fake/invisible remote and watch the world go by and change channels—this show will have people walking quickly to their destination—they are late! And this channel has young teenagers rolling by in their car, music loud, no real cares in the world except school, a cell phone bill and teen pregnancy rates. This channel will have this man, walking with his hands behind his back, taking his time, no need to rush, the end of his life may be say 25 years away but he is still going to enjoy it. To me, this is reality television.

Riding along, people seem to get distracted by the very thought of nothingness. Sure, there are IPODs and cell phones and free newspapers that make their way onto the bus but they seem to be secondary forms to distraction. Some are listening to their favorite genre of music and someone is in the middle of a lame and dull text to one of their friends describing what they are doing right at this exact moment—on bus. Lameoids. b there n 5 mins. get pot frm jimmy. I hve $20. we blazin all afternoon.

There will forever be that one person who talks louder than the others. Sure, there are no real laws saying that you have to be quiet but these people are the LNN or Loser News Network of well not only the bus and subway system but of well life itself. If anyone should write anything whether it be a book, a short story, a poem—anything—it should be them, then again, we would only be reading it as second hand news instead of getting a firsthand account of the fight they were in or the awesome time they had at this party a few nights ago or this really hot girl who just happen to be in the same convenience store as them and they were inline and struck up a 48 second conversation with her as they waited to pay for their cigarettes.

It seems like we never stop to the smell the roses anymore. We are always in motion—whether it be downloading music or fast forwarding through the commercials of a program we TiVo'd the night before—there is always motion. In the days of Hollywood and the days of faking reality television shows and the constant need for change and movement forward to something new and something better, in the days of e-commerce and e-mail and e-talk news, we are lacking in the e-motion, the movement forward of emotion and the combining of technology to make us feel better. Sure, downloading that album by the last music artist may make us feel good or watching how the latest celebrity has faltered in a major or minor way, but we seem to be spinning around in robotic circles, we lack e-motion.

How come any song I ever hear in my head when I travel is Layla by Eric Clapton? Yes, I am a fan but there are millions of other songs in the world my bPOD could be playing right now. My Shuffle button appears to be broken. Two conclusions or assumptions or conspiracy theories come to mind: It is a good song and I am a fan or the fact that I, like Eric Clapton have never met my biological father (his died in 1985). According to sources, mine is alive. Maybe there is a deep routed connection between myself and Eric Clapton based on the fact we have not met our fathers though you would think the song My Father's Eyes would be in my head, not Layla though Layla does have a good guitar riff at the intro to the song and that longish guitar solo at the end. R.I.P Duane Allman.

People just appear to getting on and off the bus at free will. Like they have no real idea where they are going. Look at people's faces right when the exit the bus or streetcar, sure they know where they are going but for that few seconds; they look lost even though they have made this journey hundreds of times before. If you got off at the wrong stop, would you wave down the bus the very second you realized you got off at the wrong stop, the feeling and the look of being lost is replaced by the feeling of stupidity on your part? We all live in fear of looking stupid. How could you get it wrong? You do this a hundred times a month? The destination has not moved in 20 years and here you are, one day, being stupid and getting off at the wrong stop. A momentary lapse of direction? Would you wave down the bus or just keep walking, looking like you know what you are doing, like you meant to get off a stop ahead of schedule and you calming read just your body motion to make it appear you are in control. I saw a man reading a Playboy in the middle of the bus, in the middle of the day once though I do not think the term "reading" applies here.

Almost at my destination. Coffee with Anna today. We have not seen each other for years. She is a good kid. She is trying her hardest in life. Boyfriend for a few years now. She lives in the next country and is in my town and country to visit. She is from Michigan, so I conclude or assume or conspiracy theory that Michiganians love to visit. In my head I just started the long Clapton/Allman guitar duet on Layla. I did not want to look stupid, so I checked the number of stops I had left before I had to get off, the correct one being in front of the coffee shop, the one I conclude, assume and conspiracy theory that all Bramptonians love going to. The loud talker seems to have settled. Even though the bus has stopped to let someone off and some more people on, I feel motion, I feel e-motion. Could it be the fact that for the first time in my life, I feel like I am the bus driver of this bus I call #32 Myself? Maybe. No more sitting in the arm chair of life, watching reality shows pass me by? Maybe.

Will the music ever change of my life CD? Sure. Though I do think if I played it backwards, there would be some good or a good message to everyone who hears it. Sure, I did some wrong in my life—who hasn't—am I ashamed of those wrongs? You bet.

Will I ever be one of those people who talk loud on the bus or subway, broadcasting my previous day's news a la LNN or BNN? Probably not but again actions speak louder than words sometimes and even though I have my hands in my pockets a lot of the time and appear to know what I am doing, deep down inside I live in a world of shyness and introvertisms and then when people ask me what my biggest fear is, it is not being alone, it is being around people. Well here I am, at the coffee shop. Anna is running late, so I sit down and wait. I had something extraordinary happen to me last night and I could not wait to share it with her. It is something that took me by surprise. Something that I never even thought to this day I had in me. A realization. A conclusion. Not that I never realize things or conclude things in my life, but this felt different. An out of body experience but in of body experience. Thought I have never done drugs, I felt that emotional high that one gets. I felt it and then I left it in the Lord's hands. She opens the door, sits down and apologizes. I open my mouth to say . . .

. . . This is the book that never ends.